CW00820850

BETSAN
THE
BRAVE

Jenny Sullivan

For Kirsty, Tanith and Stephanie,
for my nieces, nephews (great and great-great),
and also Charlotte and Harriet, with love.

J.S.

First Impression—2002

ISBN 1 84323 145 X

This book is published with the support of the
Arts Council of Wales.

Printed in Wales at
Gomer Press, Llandysul, Ceredigion

CHAPTER ONE

It *had* to be here somewhere!

The trouble with magic, Betsan thought, was that when it wasn't around any more, a person missed it.

If someone had asked her a year ago if she believed in magic, she'd probably have said, 'not really'. Unless whatever makes gorgeous flowers come out of boring little brown bulbs is magic, and snow covering the mountains and making Blaengwynfi look like a miniature version of Switzerland, is magic. But since then Betsan had met Gwydion, and her views on magic had never been the same since.

Nor had Maldwyn's. Just because Maldwyn had *thought* he was magic, he began to play rugby like a superstar! Gwydion had turned both their lives *ben-i-lawr*, topsy-turvy, and changed them for ever.

Betsan would never forget Gwydion, or the baby dragon that had followed him through the Door in Time. That was the Door that had once stood on the mountain above Blaengwynfi.

Which was where Betsan was now, wrapped up in layers of sweaters, jackets and scarves, with a woolly hat on top of it all, looking for that blooming Time Door. It *had* to be here somewhere!

The trouble was, Betsan was bored. Christmas was just over, so she felt sort of miserable and flat about that, and her friend Maldwyn had gone off on a Dragon Rugby training weekend, so she had no one to talk to. To make matters worse, her Dad had just gone back after being home for a whole month, to the far

5

away place where he worked. He wouldn't be home again for almost half a year, and she missed him badly already. Granch was Resting His Eyes, Mam was at work, and she had nothing to do except go for a climb up the Graig in the snow.

It was very cold. Her nose was so numb it might have dropped off half a mile back and she probably wouldn't even have felt it, and even through the thick socks inside her wellies her feet were getting cold. And of course, even though she'd looked and looked, the Time Door stayed determinedly hidden. That was the trouble with looking for something invisible: you couldn't see it, could you?

She found a paper hanky and wiped her nose, then shoved it back in her pocket. She *thought* she was standing just about where she'd been that summer afternoon when she'd first found the wand that had been hurled there from another time. The Time Door had been over there: she remembered the weird sensation she'd had when Gwydion was leaving. He had stepped between the two upright stones and – simply disappeared. Maldwyn had promised faithfully not to try to go through the door, but Betsan hadn't. She'd crossed her fingers behind her back, and she hadn't said a word. She *couldn't* promise not to go after an adventure, now could she? No self-respecting ten-year-old girl would do that!

Betsan gazed down on Blaengwynfi, the rows of snow-covered roofs snaking up and down the valley, the smoke twisting out of chimney-pots looking blue against the whiteness. She wasn't absolutely sure she'd go through the Door even if she found it.

6

Gwydion had warned her that terrible things lurked on the other side, but how terrible could they really be? All right, there were dragons – she knew that perfectly well, she'd met the one that followed Gwydion, hadn't she? – but surely they were either tiny, like that one, so she could run away, or they were huge, so she'd hear them and could hide, right?

If she found the door, *then* she'd decide whether or not to go through. Anyway, she certainly hadn't found it today, and inside her wellies there were two foot-shaped ice cubes, and she wanted her tea. She turned to go down the little path that wandering sheep had trodden in the snow, back to a warm fire and egg and chips. She turned back for a last glimpse at the top of the mountain, her breath smoking on the freezing air.

And suddenly, there they were.

Two tall, upright stones.

Betsan stared. The Door! She took off one of her gloves, and went and touched the left-hand stone. Her finger, even though it was purple with cold at the end, detected the faint, tinglesome shock of magic. *It was true!* The Door really was back, standing on top of the Graig, right before her very eyes.

She walked all round the stones. She could see right through to the snow-covered grass on the other side, although the air between them shimmered, rather like a tarmac road does on a hot summer day. The stones weren't very scary. There wasn't a horrible, dark tunnel or anything. She could probably pop between them, have a quick look round and pop back again before the magical stones even realised she was there. Betsan looked over her shoulder. There was no one about. How could it be dangerous just to look? Was she brave enough to risk it? Did she dare?

Of course she did! She was Betsan the Brave, wasn't she? That's what Mam always called her, usually before a visit to the dentist!

She took a deep breath, closed her eyes, crossed her fingers, and stepped quickly in between the upright stones. She expected something dramatic to happen: a mighty wind, or a terrible howling noise, even some fizzy sparks, but there was nothing at all to tell that anything had happened. Maybe nothing had. She opened one eye, expecting to see the familiar, snowy slopes of the Graig all round her.

The Graig had vanished.

Betsan was in the middle of a wood, and she was up to her knees in bluebells.

She had a quick look round, her eyes wide in amazement. She was beginning to warm up quite quickly, because she was wearing so many layers of clothing. She grinned excitedly. When Maldwyn came back next day, she could tell him that she'd been through the Time Door! He'd never believe her, of course. She'd have to convince him. But how? Then she had an idea. She bent down and picked a handful of bluebells – bluebells don't appear until late April, not ever, so showing Maldwyn bluebells in the middle of a freezing, snowy January would *certainly* convince him. Clutching the bunch of flowers, she turned to scuttle back the way she'd come, back to winter snow and safety.

But the stones weren't there any longer . . .

The bluebells dropped from her fingers. Frantically, Betsan waved her arms about, trying to feel the invisible Door-stones. She hadn't moved more than a step away from them! How could they have disappeared? She took a step forward, then another, in the hope that she might accidentally walk through them and find herself back in her own time. But she didn't.

After half an hour of feeling, and walking, and hoping, Betsan knew that, like it or not, she was stuck in some other Time. She looked around nervously, wondering where – and when – she was. The trouble with being in woods is that, while she might be able to tell that it was more or less April, the April she was in could be *anywhere at all in Time!*

Perhaps if she could find Gwydion . . . if Gwydion was *in* this Time. And what if Gwydion *was* in this Time, but this Time was *before* he'd lost Merlin's wand and he hadn't met her yet? He wouldn't know her, would he? Or what if he was in the future and so old he'd forgotten all about her? Grancher forgot lots of stuff because he was old. Betsan's brain was beginning to hurt with all the thinking. The sun was coming through the trees, dappling the bluebell wood with speckles of sunshine, and she was getting hotter and hotter.

Well, there was no point in just hanging around in the middle of a wood. She'd have to go and find out *when* she was, and *where*, but at the same time she didn't want to leave the place where the Time Door was supposed to be. Perhaps she could leave some sort of marker . . .

I know the very thing, she thought. About two tons of winter sweaters! Betsan took off her waterproof jacket and three sweaters, leaving her with just a tee shirt. Pity about the wellies, but she could hardly go tramping about in her woolly socks, could she? She made a neat pile of clothes on the spot where she thought the Time Door had been, tied the waterproof around her middle, and feeling much cooler, set off through the wood to try and find a human being.

I just hope it's a friendly one, she thought.

CHAPTER TWO

Meanwhile, not very far away, in the land of Ynys Haf (for that was the name of the strange Welsh land in Time – it means 'Island of Summer' in English), Gwydion had a half-day off from his studies with Merlin, and was trying to train a very small dragon.

While Fang, his dog from the other Time, was quite obedient, and (if he felt like it) would sit, or fetch, or stay when Gwydion commanded, Gwydion had discovered that dragons were a different prospect altogether.

The trouble with dragons is that they are very independent and rather stubborn creatures, probably because after a few centuries, they become very, very large, and so very, very few people are inclined to disagree with them, still less order them about. But as everyone knows, if a person gets a baby dragon straight out of the egg, and takes time to train it properly, dragons make wonderful pets. A baby dragon will curl on your lap like a kitten until it gets too big and spiky, and then it can make a great footstool, (except for the spikes, which are a bit uncomfortable on your toeses). Dragons are excellent at lighting fires, toasting toast, and in summer they are quite happy to lie on their backs and play barbecue, so that (if sausages and burgers had been invented) you could have fried them easily. They also make amazing house-guards, because by the time a burglar realises that there is a watch-dragon in the house, it's much too late for the burglar. There's nothing left of *him* except a pair of smoking boots . . .

But, as Gwydion was discovering, it's *training* them that is the difficult part.

'Sit, Bugsy!' he commanded. Bugsy nonchalantly lifted his front paw and inspected his talons. He nibbled one that was getting a bit blunt until it was a nice, sharp point again.

'I said, *sit*, Bugsy!' Gwydion repeated, more firmly this time. Bugsy ambled over to a rose-bush and fried it.

'Oh, *rats,*' Gwydion said. Now there would be trouble. That rose-bush was Merlin's favourite. It was a Hybrid Tea Rose and it hadn't been invented yet. Merlin had brought it back from the twenty-first century, had fed it all sorts of fertilisers, pruned it, watered it, and it had just bloomed for the very first time.

Gwydion inspected the charred stem. Well, it certainly wouldn't bloom again, ever. He sighed. There was no point in ticking Bugsy off. He was just doing what dragons did. However, he thought it would be a good idea if he and Bugsy and Fang took themselves off somewhere else. Then, if Merlin came out to inspect his beloved rose he *might* think someone else's dragon was responsible. Then again, he might not.

Whistling for the two creatures to follow, Gwydion set off towards the woods. Fang bounded ahead, shoving his nose into every bush and rabbit-hole. Gwydion thought of calling him to heel in case he shoved his nose into a dragon-nest, but there again, if he got his nose scorched, he'd learn a lesson and wouldn't do it again. Bugsy followed, not because

12

Gwydion had whistled, but because he felt like going for a bit of a fly. He flapped overhead, amusing himself by huffing fire at passing birds to make them squawk, and shrivelling up bits of tree.

Suddenly Fang stopped dead. He whined and ran round in circles beneath a large bush. Gwydion caught up with him.

'What, Fang?' he asked, patting the dog's head.

'Whimper!' Fang said, meaning 'Look!'

'What are you fussing about?' Gwydion said.

'Rowrff!' Fang said, which was perfectly understandable to anyone who spoke Dog. '*Will* you *look* when I tell you!'

'What is it, chum? Is it a rabbit?'

'Werrrfff,' Fang said disgustedly, which as I'm sure you know, means 'Oh, good grief!' Gathering his hindquarters beneath him he jumped in the air as high as he could reach, and just managed to prod the branch with his nose.

Something fell off it. Something yellow and shiny.

'What on earth is that?' Gwydion wondered aloud, bending down.

About blooming time too! Fang thought. These humans took an awful lot of training. Still, they weren't very bright to start with, so a dog couldn't expect too much of them, and *his* human seemed to be one of the more intelligent ones!

Gwydion picked up the object. Fang knew perfectly well what it was, and even whose it was, by the smell. He wondered how long it would take Gwydion to work it out.

It took quite a while. So long, in fact, that Fang

13

curled up in a ball and went to sleep, and Bugsy wandered off to annoy a squirrel.

Gwydion turned the thing over in his hand. He'd seen something like it before, but where? It was a butterfly, made of some hard, shiny stuff that he recognised, but it certainly wasn't from this Time. The butterfly was bright yellow, and had glittery stuff all over its wings. It wasn't a real butterfly, but it was a pretty good pretend one. Gwydion rubbed his fingertips over the wings to see if the glitter was magic. Nope. No tingle, just a gritty feeling. The butterfly was attached to a loop of yellow stuff. Gwydion tried to pull it off, but the material just stretched. Now this was getting annoying. He knew exactly what it was – but what was it?

Then he noticed that, caught in the stretchy bit, was a long, brown human hair. *Got it!* he thought. *It's one of those things Betsan used to tie up her hair behind her head.* He remembered now. That was one mystery solved. The other was just beginning. Where had the stretchy butterfly thing come from? It had no right at all in this Time. And it had been caught on a branch at exactly the height that a not-very-tall person might have been wearing it in their hair . . .

'Fang?' he said at last, prodding the rottweiler gently with his toe, and putting the hair-thing under his nose, 'seek!'

You took your time! Fang thought, getting up and stretching. *All you had to do was ask, mate!*

Fang took another deep sniff of the hair-thing, put his nose to the ground, and set off. He could have gone straight to what he could smell, but to pay

Gwydion back for being so slow, and to teach him to hurry up next time, Fang took him the long way round.

Then, in the middle of a sun-dappled wood full of sapphire bluebells, Fang relented and showed Gwydion what he had been looking for.

A large pile of clothes on the ground.

On the ground rather close to where a Time Door usually Was.

But sometimes Wasn't.

Gwydion stooped and sorted through the clothes. He'd seen clothes like this before. Cold weather clothes. Big woollen tunics. Long pieces of cloth to wrap round necks. Round woollen hats. Stripy hand-covers, with a space for every finger. He picked up one of the tunics and examined it closely. Sewn inside the neck, at the back, was a tiny piece of white cloth. A name was written on it, in red writing.

Betsan M. Price

it said.

Gwydion's knees gave way. He sat on a bluebell and squashed it. 'Oops, sorry, bluebell!' he said, getting up quickly and mending it (even plants have feelings in Ynys Haf).

He looked around. Because he was magic, he could see the image of the Time Door, even though it wasn't there. (If you find that hard to understand, try looking at an electric light for a second, and then close your eyes. Even though your eyes are shut, you can still see the light, right? Well, that's how Gwydion can see Time Doors that aren't there. OK now? Great. On with the story.)

15

Despite Fang's opinion of his intelligence, Gwydion was really quite clever, which is why it didn't take him very long at all to work out that he had a Very Big Problem.

Betsan Price had somehow found the Time Door and was loose in Ynys Haf. And if Merlin found out about *that,* there would be Trouble with a capital T.

For Gwydion.

Gwydion knew, because there was only one set of clothes, that only Betsan had managed to get through. Maldwyn had stayed behind, which was one good thing. Besides, Gwydion distinctly remembered Maldwyn promising never, ever, to go through a Time Door if he found one, but now that he thought about it, Gwydion realised that Betsan hadn't promised anything . . .

Oh, no! Betsan couldn't *begin* to understand the dangers in this Time! Apart from all the magic that was lying about all over the place, there were Ravening Wolves, for a start. Huge Fiery Dragons. Giants. Wild boars. Tylwyth Teg, fairies that were sometimes good fairies, but more often weren't. And there was also the Great Druid, who rather fancied himself as a bit of a wizard himself – but he wasn't very good at it, so he cheated. Luckily, Merlin had trapped him in a cave somewhere, so maybe Betsan didn't need to worry about him after all.

There was only one thing to do. Gwydion had to find Betsan before anything at all happened to her, and send her back to her own Time, fast.

CHAPTER THREE

Betsan headed off down a small path leading through the wood. It was such a small, narrow path it had probably been made by rabbits rather than people, and it had a nasty habit of disappearing under brambles that she had to fight her way around, so quite quickly she was covered in scratches. Of course, she was still a stranger to the wood, it hadn't got to know her yet, and so the wood was behaving in an altogether wood-ish manner, which it was perfectly entitled to do. Once she left the pleasant, bluebell bit behind, however, the wood got darker, deeper, and rather more sinister, and once or twice she got a nasty feeling that someone – or something – was watching her.

She turned round quickly, but there was never anybody there. Still, she couldn't quite shake off the feeling that she wasn't alone. The wood became thicker and thicker, and the sunlight got through less and less, and after a while what was left of the light had a sort of greenish, underwater look to it. Betsan stopped walking and looked around her. She was beginning to feel nervous: she still had the 'someone's watching' feeling, but she could see no one. She was feeling hot and tired now, and had begun to stumble over fallen branches and slither on patches of mud. At last she found a fallen tree and sat on it.

'Now, Betsan M Price,' she said firmly, 'get a grip on yourself. Pull yourself together. You are Betsan the Brave, this is only a wood,' *(a very deep wood,* a voice inside her head told her, *probably with Scary Things in*

17

it) 'and all woods must come to an end somewhere. So get your breath back and –'

She didn't finish the lecture she was giving herself. She didn't finish it because suddenly, the ground began to shake, and at the same time she heard a rhythmic thumping that was so loud her teeth rattled. The log she was sitting on juddered up and down with each thump, and Betsan looked around in alarm.

Then, as well as the thumping (it was like one of those hammer things that road-menders used to flatten the road out – a pile-driver, that was it!), she heard the unmistakable sound of splintering, groaning wood. It sounded as if the forest were being ripped apart, tree by tree. The thumping got louder, and the jolts coming up through the log got so violent and uncomfortable that Betsan stood up before her bottom got bruised. She looked all round, trying to see what was making the sound and the vibration. It was getting closer, but still she couldn't see anyth –

Then she could. A huge hand appeared above her at tree-top height, caught a branch half-way down the tree right next to her, and ripped it off. The branch was about as round as Betsan's middle . . . Then a bare knee the size of an elephant poked between them, closely followed by the rest of the –

Giant.

Betsan's brain went numb. *There. Are. No. Such. Things. As. Giants*, she told herself. The unexpected heat must have addled her brain or something. She closed her eyes, hoping that by the time she opened them again, the giant would be Not There. She opened them. Wrong again. The Giant was most definitely

There. Belatedly, Betsan decided it would be a good idea to run. Her wellies slithered and slid in the muddy patches between the trees as she made off in the general direction of Elsewhere. She hoped she was small enough that the giant wouldn't notice her, the way humans didn't always notice ants. She felt like an ant. She just hoped the giant wouldn't tread on her.

It didn't. Instead, Betsan's world suddenly went very, very dark. The giant had reached out an arm and put his cupped hand down over her. She kicked frantically at his fingers, trying to get free, but it was a bit like kicking a telegraph pole. It hurt.

The giant fingers slowly, gently, closed, holding her loosely in his fist. Betsan's stomach lurched as she rose quickly through the air. Then she was jumbled about, and another gigantic hand joined the first, so that she was cupped between the two rough palms. The vast thumbs parted, and a huge blue eye peered in at her. Betsan cowered.

'Don't hurt me,' she squeaked, completely forgetting to be Betsan the Brave. 'I don't mean any harm, honest.'

The giant's head drew back and she was able to see the whole face. It was showing teeth, each one the size of a television set, and Betsan suddenly realised that it was smiling.

Then a great rumbling vibration began, and the hands holding Betsan began to shake violently, tumbling her about like dice in a cup. He was laughing!

'How could you harm me, little thing?' it boomed at her, and Betsan put both hands over her ears.

19

'Ow! Don't shout!' she complained.

'Sorry!' the giant said in a loud whisper. 'Didn't mean to be shoutsome at you!'

Betsan began to feel better. Maybe it wasn't a fee-fi-fo-fum sort of giant. Maybe it wouldn't eat her or squash her. She got her balance on the huge hand and put her head back to look up at him.

'It's really nice to meet you,' she said, 'but do you think you could put me down so that I can go? I really need to find someone.'

The giant looked crestfallen. 'Doesn't you like me?' it asked. 'I like you! I doesn't know what you is, but I like you!'

'Of course I like you,' Betsan said quickly, 'only I'm a bit busy today. Maybe we could meet up again some other time?'

The giant looked even sadder. 'I were wanting to play with you,' he said mournfully. 'Nobody ever got time to play with I. Mammy don't, Dada don't, Mam-gu don't.' He sat disconsolately on a log, the thump as he sat down jerking Betsan off her feet again.

Mammy? Dada? Mam-gu? Betsan thought. She stared at the giant. 'Don't mind me asking,' she said, 'but how old are you?'

'Seventy-two,' the giant said sadly. 'An' everyone says "go away little boy". "Don't go bothering, little boy". "Busy now, little boy".' He sighed, and the wind almost knocked Betsan over. 'Don't nobody not never got time to play with I. I is lonesome.'

'That's rotten,' Betsan said sympathetically, wondering how old a giant seventy-two was in human age. About five from the sound of him. 'I really feel sorry for you. It's awful when nobody's got time to play, isn't it? But I really need to get going.'

The giant stuck its bottom lip out. 'No. I gonna keep you. Then I have somebody to talk to. I gonna keep you in my pocket. You gonna be my pet.'

'Nooo!' Betsan shrieked, but it was too late. A large pocket had been opened, and Betsan was dropped in. If you imagine a pocket the size of a bed sheet, you might get some idea. It was hot in the pocket, there was a sticky boiled sweet the size of a dust-bin lid at the bottom, all covered in fluff, and when the giant set off for wherever he was going, Betsan had to cling on to the fabric as hard as she could.

Once the giant got into his stride, it wasn't too bad. After a while she let herself slip to the bottom of the pocket (she kicked the sweet out of the way) and it felt a bit like being in a hammock. She didn't feel relaxed enough to sleep, however. He might be a small giant, and reasonably friendly, but the Mammy and the Dada might be quite different.

The giant footsteps slowed and stopped. There was the sound of a door opening. A very large door. Betsan crouched down in the pocket, feeling very, very scared.

'Mammy? Is you home?'

'Where else would a Mammy be?' a thunderous voice boomed. 'Always clothes to wash, floors to scrub, food to cook. Always busy, busy, busy! All right for your Dada, he can go off seven-league-booting it all over the place, but I'm stuck here cleaning, washing, ironing, cooking, never go anywhere, I don't.'

21

'Mammy, guess what I found –' Betsan's captor began, still whispering so that he wouldn't hurt Betsan's ears.

'Whatever it is, I've got no time to look at it now,' the vast voice boomed. 'And it's time for your nap.'

'Aw, Mammy, does I got to nap?' the young giant complained. 'I isn't tired one bit!'

'Bed! Now!' bellowed the other voice. Betsan almost felt sorry for her giant – it didn't feel like a very happy family, somehow. With a deep sigh, Betsan's giant began to move, and she clung on to the pocket again. She heard another door open and close, and then there was a strange sensation, rather like going down a hundred floors in a very fast lift. A thud, a few sighs, a grumble or two, and everything was still. Everything was quiet. Then . . .

'Groowwwfffff-whisssssstle. Grooooowwff-whisss-sstle. Snort.'

Betsan listened, puzzled. Then it dawned on her. *He was snoring!*

Carefully, she clambered to the top of the pocket and peered out. She looked up. Sure enough, the huge head nestled on a pillow, the huge mouth was open, the eyes were tight shut and the giant was fast asleep.

Betsan scrambled out of the pocket in a flash. She clambered down the giant's shirt, ran across to the edge of the bed and clambered down the counterpane to the floor. It was like abseiling down a mountainside!

The door was so huge that she was able to crawl through the gap beneath, then she hid against the wall and looked around her. She was in a room the size of a

22

cathedral, and in the middle of the floor a female giant twice the size of Betsan's captor was stirring something in a vast pot. Luckily, her back was turned towards the bedroom where her enormous child lay napping, and Betsan took the opportunity to shoot off like a terrified rabbit towards the open door of the house.

Outside, she headed for the trees. The wood that had seemed so threatening now looked like the safest haven imaginable, and Betsan hardly dared breathe until she was in the shelter of its trees. She didn't stop running, though. On she went until, at last, the trees began to be spaced further apart, and Betsan knew that she was coming to the end of the wood.

CHAPTER FOUR

It was quite surprising, really, that Gwydion didn't notice the giant. But it was a very big wood, and giants weren't really that much of a novelty for Gwydion, who had grown up with them. They were slowly becoming extinct, though this was partly because in Olden Times they had been hunted quite a lot, and partly because in the present Time the few remaining giants were argumentative and didn't get on with each other at all well. They spent so much time fighting among themselves that they could hardly raise a 'fee-fi-fo-fum' even for the blood of an Englishman!

No, Gwydion was busily setting off in entirely the wrong direction. He shoved Betsan's bobble-hat in his pocket and decided that the sooner he found Betsan the better it would be for all concerned. The last thing he wanted was for Merlin to find out that a human had managed to sneak through the Time Door. He shuddered to think what his master would do if he knew.

Fang and Bugsy followed Gwydion, feeling confused. They wondered where in Ynys Haf this idiot was going, and if he was looking for the human, why was he going this way when it was perfectly obvious (at least to Fang, who had picked up Betsan's scent long ago) that she was heading in completely the opposite direction.

'Come on, you two!' Gwydion panted, crashing through the undergrowth. 'Keep up, can't you!'

Fang and Bugsy exchanged Looks again. They were getting very good at Looks. This particular Look said, 'Who wants to keep up when, just around that bush, there's a very large, very ferocious, wild boar?'

Now, you might think that a wild boar is just another name for a gentleman wild pig, but you'd be wrong. Wild boars in this Time were medieval boars: they were hunted by humans, and unlike a lot of human prey, they quite often got their own back on them – first, if you see what I mean. Wild boars were equipped with ginormous tusks, humungous teeth, sharp hooves and quite the nastiest disposition of any creature (including bears, of which there were quite a number also) in the forest.

But there went Gwydion, blundering through the trees and bushes, not keeping his eyes open at all. And then he was round the bush, and Gwydion and the boar were boy-eyeball to red piggy-eyeball.

Gwydion skidded to a halt. 'Oops!' he said, walking backwards very quickly so as not to take his eyes off the boar. Bugsy flew up and Fang disappeared into a badger's sett. The sett, fortunately, was disused, because an angry badger would have been something to be reckoned with, too.

The boar pawed the ground and snorted. It fixed its little, savage eyes on Gwydion and lowered its head. It thought about charging. It thought about charging REALLY FAST and digging his tusks into Gwydion's ankles so that he fell over. Then he thought about charging and ripping and goring and generally making Gwydion resemble minced beef. (Except that it wouldn't have known what that is, of course). It decided to act on its thoughts.

Luckily for Gwydion, the boar was a slow thinker

and an even slower decider. By the time the thought had turned into a decision, and the decision had reached the bad-tempered little brain, and the bad-tempered little brain had sent a message to the hooves and the tusks and the legs and stuff, Gwydion had gone up a tree like a terrified squirrel. Fortunately, wild boars can't climb trees, so after snorting and kicking, charging the trunk so that the tree shook, stamping and squealing and swearing, shouting 'Come down and fight, you rotten coward' in boar-talk and generally acting in a boarish fashion at the foot of the tree, it wandered off in search of other prey.

Gwydion thought about climbing down. He decided to wait a bit. Bugsy curled up on a branch next to him, and Fang cautiously emerged from the badger's sett.

After the sounds of the boar's passing had disappeared in the distance, Gwydion thought again about climbing down. The trouble was, fear had got him up there: he didn't think he could have got up there any other way but jet-propelled by pure terror. But now he was safe, he noticed how smooth the trunk was. How very few branches grew up its sides. How almost impossible it was going to be to climb down . . .

Bugsy, of course, very soon got bored and hungry and flew down. Fang sat about at the bottom of the tree for a while waiting for his human to join him. After several attempts, several failures and lots of patches of skin missing from elbows, knees and shins, Gwydion gave up.

'Fang?' he called, and the dog looked up. 'Good boy. Go and fetch someone, Fang. Tell them I'm stuck up a tree, right?'

26

Fang understood perfectly. The trouble was, he didn't talk Person, did he? So even if he found someone, how was he going to get them to understand that Gwydion was stuck up a tree? Honestly, what was Gwydion *like?* Didn't he have a brain at all?

'Go on, Fang, good boy!' Gwydion urged from his perch in the tree.

Well, Fang thought, *a nod's as good as a wink to a blind man*. He wasn't quite sure what that meant, but it sounded good. So he and Bugsy went hunting for rabbits to pass the time.

Gwydion could have been stuck up there forever, except for a sort of a happy accident.

Remember the little giant? The one who wanted to keep Betsan to play with? Well, when he woke up, he looked in his pocket, and discovered that his new toy had legged it. Because he wasn't a very old giant, he was upset at this. He threw a tantrum that was alarming to behold. He stamped out of his bedroom, out of the house into the forest, uprooted trees and threw them, stamped on boulders and crushed them into powder, screamed and cried and generally behaved like a five-year-old, which he sort of was. Then he decided to go home again and pester his Mammy, and the way home just happened to go past the tree that Gwydion was hiding in.

Gwydion heard him coming – it would have been difficult not to, because he sounded like a vast herd of elephants stampeding. He felt the ground – and the tree he was stuck in – begin to shake and shudder as the giant got closer and closer. From his vantage point in the tree he saw the path that the giant was taking by

27

the way the trees bent and swayed and sailed through the air. Gwydion wrapped his arms and legs round the trunk of his tree and hung on for dear life. And then the giant was upon him. Gwydion shut his eyes and hung on harder. Just his luck to run up against one of the few remaining giants!

His tree shook. His tree swayed from side to side alarmingly, bending like a stalk of wheat before a mighty wind. The giant lashed out bad-temperedly at the tree-top, and the tree cracked and split halfway down, folding like a broken matchstick. Gwydion hung on – upside down – like a koala bear or a three-toed sloth, and waited until the giant's stamping receded in the distance. And then it was quiet again.

Gwydion opened his eyes. Fang had crept back and was sitting with his nose about two inches away from Gwydion's upside-down one. Gwydion's head was about six inches from the ground.

He'd been hanging on so tightly that it took him a while to get his arms and legs to understand that they could let go now. But eventually they did, and Gwydion collapsed in a heap on the mass of broken twigs and ripped off branches that had once been a tree.

He sat up, shakily, and retrieved Betsan's bobble hat from his pocket. Wild boars, giants, and still there was Betsan to find.

'Come on, guys,' he said.

CHAPTER FIVE

It was a huge relief for Betsan to find herself with open country in front of her. She'd be able to see any giants coming long before they spotted her.

Wherever she was, it certainly wasn't Blaengwynfi. The land sloped away from her, a gentle green downhill curve, and became a small valley heading into a V-shape of wooded hills. Framed in the V was a blue mass that could only be the sea, and a small stream ambled happily down the hill beside her, minding its own business. Wherever she was, she was facing west – the sun was sitting like a giant crimson ball on the sea, painting the waves with flame. Even as she watched she noticed that the bottom edge of the sun was disappearing below the horizon. When it disappeared altogether, it would be dark.

And Betsan had nowhere to go. Nowhere to sleep.

Not yet I haven't, she thought. So, start looking, Betsan! She hoped Mam and Granch wouldn't worry when she didn't come home. Fat chance of that. Mam would have the Police, Mountain Rescue and probably Superman, Batman and Wonderwoman out looking as soon as she realised Betsan was missing. There'd be ructions when she got back. If she got back. After the encounter with the giant she wasn't quite as confident as she had been.

Betsan pushed that thought aside, and set off down the hill. Perhaps she could find a cottage with a friendly person inside. Someone who could give her something to eat and a bed for the night, perhaps.

29

Perhaps the someone could tell her where to find Gwydion, who would probably be furious with her for venturing through the Time Door, but who would eventually forgive her and help her go home.

It was getting very dark indeed when Betsan saw the cottage. It was very small, and from a distance, it looked quite sweet with its thatched roof, low, square door and two little windows covered with wooden shutters. It didn't have a chimney, but smoke wandered out of a hole in the thatch. When she got close, Betsan could see that the walls were very thick. She went up to the door and raised her hand to knock. And stopped.

Into her head popped an illustration from a picture book she'd had when she'd been really small. It had been the story of Hansel and Gretel and there had been a picture of a cottage *just like this*. And living in that cottage was a wicked old witch with a hooked nose and an up-curved chin, and a pointy hat and warts. There'd been an iron cage in the corner of the picture, and the wicked witch had locked Hansel and Gretel in the cage and was boiling up a cauldron of water ready to cook and eat them.

Now, Betsan is a twenty-first century kid, just like you, and she really didn't believe in witches. But then, she hadn't believed in magic, either, until she'd met Gwydion, and now she was in Gwydion's country, and now she stopped to think about it, up close the cottage looked quite sinister and not at all welcoming. Betsan decided not to knock, and began to tiptoe away.

But then a gleam of light caught her eye, shining from a knot-hole in the wooden shutter covering the window. She crept up beneath the window, waited a while, and then slowly, carefully, put her eye to the hole.

She couldn't see much. Some wooden furniture, some curious things like thin, tall candles stuck in wooden holders, a Welsh dresser with some shining pewter dishes on – and then, into the small area of the inside of the room that she could see, wandered a woman. Betsan let out a huge sigh of relief. No way could she be a witch!

She was tall and slim and blonde and pretty. And she wore a floaty dress of rosy pink. Whoever heard of a witch in pink? Besides, she had a dear little turned-up nose, huge blue eyes and rosebud lips. Snow White, possibly. *Wicked witch? Not on your nelly,* thought Betsan. So she knocked on the door and the beautiful creature opened it, a sweet smile curving her lips.

'I'm sorry to bother you,' Betsan began, smiling back, 'but I'm lost, and I wondered if you could possibly be kind enough to give me a place to sleep for the night?' She didn't like to ask for something to eat, although she was absolutely starving.

The beautiful smile grew wider, showing perfectly white, even teeth. There wasn't a wart in sight, and her skin was just like a rose petal.

'But of course, you dear, sweet, pretty child! Come in at once, and welcome to my humble little home!' Her voice tinkled like tiny bells.

Betsan stepped across the threshhold, and the woman shut the door behind her. The room was clean, gleaming, welcoming. A bunch of wildflowers stood in an earthenware jug and a small, bright bird sang in

31

a cage. A roaring fire burned under a small pot from which fragrant steam rose. 'Will you have some hot broth to warm you?' she tinkled, still smiling sweetly.

Actually, Betsan would have preferred a cool drink of water, and a piece of bread and butter, but it seemed rude to turn down the hot broth since it was offered, so she took the wooden bowl and spoon and sat down on a stool to eat. The woman bustled about getting a mattress thing from a platform in the eaves that was reached by a little ladder, and putting a pile of sheepskins on to it.

'You shall sleep in my bed,' she trilled, 'and I shall sleep down here.'

'I don't want to be any trouble,' Betsan protested. 'Please, let me sleep down here. I don't want to turn you out of your own bed.'

'Oh, don't worry your dear, sweet little head about it!' the woman said, watching Betsan with her bright blue eyes (rather like a Barbie doll, Betsan thought, and then felt guilty because the woman was being so kind).

'If you're certain,' Betsan said, and when her broth was all gone, she wished the woman goodnight and climbed up the precarious ladder to the sleeping platform. She snuggled down on the pallet, pulled a warm sheepskin over her shoulders, and tried to sleep.

The trouble was, she couldn't. For a start, she had a horrible suspicion that there might be fleas in the sheepskin. Something was crawling over her tummy, and she had a definite feeling that it was biting her. She was itching. Besides, the sheepskin was hot, and even though she was so exhausted, she ached all over, and she just couldn't seem to get to sleep. Anyway, even though it was dark outside, it was still early and nowhere near her bed-time.

She wriggled to the edge of the sleeping platform and peeped over. The woman wasn't lying beside the fire, sleeping. She was bending over a big wooden chest that stood in the darkest corner of the room, almost completely hidden in the shadows.

Betsan looked around the room. She hadn't really looked before. The woman's blue eyes had somehow held hers, and then there had been the steam from the delicious broth, that had made her eyes blur, and so she hadn't noticed much.

She hadn't noticed the cauldron, bubbling over the fire in the middle of the room, for a start. It wasn't the pot the broth had come from. She hadn't noticed the dark cloak and tall, pointy hat hanging on the back of the door, either, or the night-black cat stretched out beside the fire, yawning lazily, showing needle teeth in its pink cavern of a mouth. She hadn't noticed the old-fashioned broomstick leaning in a corner, or the huge book open on a table that looked for all the world like a spell book . . .

Betsan's brain suddenly went, 'ping!' Just like that: 'ping!' It was a bit like a kitchen timer reminding you that your boiled eggs are cooked. Only this 'ping' was saying, *cauldron, cloak, pointy hat, black cat, broomstick, spell-book – HELP!*

Betsan suddenly felt even less like sleeping. She was wide awake, and panicking. The woman closed the lid of the big chest in the corner and moved into the yellowish glow of the tall candle-things.

She wasn't pretty any more!

Just as if Betsan had put on magic glasses, everything looked different. The blue, Barbie-doll eyes were hooded by heavy, black eyebrows that jutted over a hooked nose and an up-curved chin. A fine crop of hairy warts sprouted all over the woman's face, and greasy, straggly hair wisped across her bony skull. The sweetly-singing caged bird was a huge, evil-looking raven, and the cottage was filled with cobwebs and dirt. The rank smell of the candles turned her stomach. The woman hadn't noticed Betsan peeping, but the cat watched her with malicious green eyes.

A curious sound rose up to Betsan's ears. The woman was singing.

> *Pound and a half of juicy bat-ears*
> *Ripe frogs' eyeballs, snagwort and poo*
> *Thirty-three grams of crocodile toe-nails*
> *And pitiful human, that finishes YOU!*

Betsan's stomach lurched. She'd done it now! Walked straight into a witch's house and *asked* for it. She had to get out of there, fast! She looked around her in panic. There was no way out of the house from up here unless she broke through the thatch, and she didn't think she could do that, it was too thick. She looked over the edge of the platform again. The cat saw her, blinked, and lazily stretched out a paw, its dagger claws extended, and the witch glanced up. Instantly, the Barbie-doll was back.

'Oh, you dear, sweet child,' she said sweetly, in her silvery bell-voice, 'can't you sleep?'

34

Betsan suddenly had an idea. If only it would work. 'No, I can't,' she said, trying to smile as if everything was perfectly all right when it wasn't, not at all. 'I forgot to go to the loo before I came up. I'm sorry, I'm going to have to go outside.'

'The loo?' the woman said, frowning prettily. 'What is the loo?'

'I need a –' What *was* the medieval word for 'wee'? She decided to try that one, and the woman smiled and nodded.

'Come down, my dear, and I'll give you a lantern,' she said. 'It's very dark out there, and there are nasty, horrible creatures about at night. I shouldn't like anything bad to happen to you.'

Me, neither! Betsan thought as she scuttled down the ladder, took the lantern and opened the cottage door. As she closed it behind her she noticed that the room was gleaming again, and the songbird was back in the raven's cage . . .

Outside she wandered a little way off, and glanced back. Sure enough, she could see the woman's silhouette peering out of the shuttered window. She was watching her. Betsan gave a little wave and disappeared behind a tree. She hung the lantern on a nearby bush, gave it a little push to distract the witch's eyes, and ran for her life.

CHAPTER SIX

Gwydion held Betsan's woolly hat under Fang's nose. Bugsy watched with interest as the dog took a big sniff. He fluttered down from the tree he was perched in, and sat beside his master. He wasn't sure what was going on, but it looked as if it might be more interesting than the silly 'Sit' game. What was so special about sitting, anyway? Flying was much more fun, and there were much more interesting things to do than *sitting,* for goodness sake. Like creeping up behind the Merlin-Master and frizzling his shoelaces. That had *really* annoyed him last time Bugsy had done it. Bugsy quite enjoyed annoying Merlin – even though he always made certain his escape route was clear first!

Fang closed his eyes and breathed deeply. He could smell the Betsan-smell very strongly. He took his nose out of the hat and sniffed the grass. There it was again. She'd definitely gone in *that* direction.

'Got it, Fang?' Gwydion asked. 'Can you find her, boy?'

Fang sighed. Of course he could. Betsan's signal was so clear that it almost shone, like a snail-trail on a summer morning. The question was, would he take Gwydion the direct way, or would he take him the long way round, just for the fun of it?

'Oh, come on, you dumb dog!' Gwydion muttered impatiently. The trouble with Gwydion was that he didn't realise that Fang understood every single word . . .

That did it. *Right, you! Fang thought crossly. For that, you go the long way round! Teach you a bit of respect.*

Which was why, as the sun went down, just as Betsan was knocking timidly on the witch's cottage door, Gwydion was only about a hundred metres from where he'd started. Fang had led him into a thorn-bush, through a hollow tree, through a patch of mud so sticky that he'd lost one of his boots, and rather too close to a wild bees' nest (Bugsy had investigated that: he loved honey, and his scales meant he never got stung. *Bugsy* didn't get stung, but the bees were very cross, and so Gwydion did. Five times.)

It was getting dark by this time, and Castell Du, with Merlin's tower jutting up above the battlements, shone through the darkness as the lanterns and candles inside it were lighted.

'It's no good looking for Betsan in the dark,' Gwydion said worriedly. 'We might as well go home for the night and start again tomorrow.' Which was fine by Fang and Bugsy. They were both hungry.

So they went home and ate an excellent supper, managing to avoid Merlin, who'd popped off to a Wizards' Conference somewhere in the future. Just about the time Betsan was running for her life through the night woods, Gwydion, Bugsy and Fang, curled up in a warm, untidy heap on Gwydion's bed, all fell asleep.

Gwydion woke to discover that Merlin was back. Not only was he back, but he had gone out to visit his favourite rosebush, and discovered that it had been barbecued.

Merlin was not a happy Magician. He stormed into Gwydion's room – the other boys Gwydion shared with speedily made themselves scarce when they saw the expression on the Master's face – and he grabbed the edge of Gwydion's mattress and heaved.

Gwydion flew out of bed, landed with a thump on the floor, and woke up very fast. Fang and Bugsy, realising that Merlin so early in the morning could only mean Trouble, slithered out of the room in search of breakfast.

'You, you, you – you *boy* you!' Merlin spluttered. 'What have you done to my roses, you good-for-nothing wretch? All that work and you let that nasty little creature of yours burn it! I should turn you into an ice-floe and melt you! I should turn you into a slug and put salt on you! I should send you back to your father and simply *refuse* to attempt to teach you magic, ever again! You useless lump, get out of bed!'

'I am out of bed, Merlin,' Gwydion mumbled, fighting his way out of his bed-covers.

'And have you cleaned out that cupboard I told you to empty before I left yesterday?'

Gwydion shook his head, and ducked as a thunderbolt rattled off the chest beside his head.

'Have you emptied out those spell-bottles without the labels and washed them?'

Gwydion shook his head, and dodged as a ribbon of fire shot past his nose and out of the turret window.

'Have you cleaned out the mice cage? Sorted that batch of crocodile toenails? Grated the unicorn horn?'

Gwydion shook his head, and Merlin let out such a roar of rage that the whole tower trembled and dust flew from between the stones.

'Then all your days off are cancelled until you are

38

at least THREE HUNDRED!' Merlin roared. 'You are going NOWHERE until ALL THOSE CHORES ARE DONE!'

'Yes, Merlin,' Gwydion said, glumly. He'd been planning on getting some of the boys to practise playing bugsy on Saturday. He almost had two teams, now, and he was planning on setting up a Dragon Bugsy Tournament. He'd managed to squash a pig's bladder into sort of the right oval shape for a bugsy ball, but if Merlin wasn't letting him out until he was three hundred, then –'

Then he remembered Betsan.

'But –!' he wailed, but Merlin's glare stopped him. The Master's eyes were red as glowing coals, and they sort of pinned Gwydion to the floor.

'But?' Merlin said in a spine-chilling growl. 'Did I hear you say "buuuuutttt"?'

'No-sir,' Gwydion said, shaking his head firmly. 'No buts, sir, none at all, sir, no-sir.'

'Goooood!' Merlin said in a dangerous voice. 'When you have done all the tasks I set you weeks ago, you can come and report to me. And they are NOT to be done by magic, or you will do them all over again. And they are NOT to be skimped and scamped, or you will do them again until they are perfect. And when you've done them,' he bellowed, 'I'LL FIND YOU SOME MORE JOBS TO DO!'

And Merlin swept out of the room, leaving Gwydion's ears ringing like bells.

'Oh, heck,' Gwydion said miserably. 'That's torn it!'

Bugsy and Fang slithered back into the room once it was safe again. Gwydion petted Fang's ears

39

listlessly. 'I'm stuck, Fang!' he groaned. 'If I set one hair of my head outside the tower I'm for it. He'll probably turn me into something small and slimy until I'm too old to care. And Betsan's out there somewhere. Goodness knows what trouble she'll get into.'

Bugsy Looked at Fang and Fang Looked at Bugsy. They didn't speak the same language, since Bugsy (of course) spoke Dragon, and Fang (naturally) spoke Dog. But they both spoke Look. And the Look that passed between them said in both Dragon and Dog, 'He may be stuck here, but we're not! We can find Betsan, right?'

So Dragon and Dog left their master glumly cleaning out a cupboard full of long-lost spells and dusty pots of newts' eyelashes, slugslime, crushed snailshell and assorted cans of baked beans and pineapple and tuna-fish that were absolutely useless until someone invented a can opener, and went looking for Betsan.

Fang followed her trail on the ground, his powerful nose sniff-sniffing along the scent she had left, and Bugsy flew above his head, not bothering to annoy anything at all along the way. This time, Fang went straight as an arrow wherever Betsan had been. He didn't bother to go through bogs and hollow trees, he just followed his nose straight to:

The Witch's cottage.

When he realised where Betsan had gone, he put his head in his paws and groaned. Bugsy moaned sadly. This was bad. Humans and witches didn't mix. Goodness knows what might have happened to her.

She might already have been turned into a toad or a worm or something.

Bugsy was tempted to set fire to the witch's thatched roof, but Betsan might still be in there, and he didn't want her to be hurt. He flew to the window and peered in. The witch was inside: because Bugsy was magic, naturally the witch looked exactly as she always did.

She looked very, very ugly. Remarkably evil. Positively scarifying, even to a dragon. She couldn't fool him, and she couldn't fool Fang, who could smell a witch half a mile away.

Bugsy's keen eyes suddenly caught movement on the grimy table in the middle of the cottage's earthen floor. Sitting in a large glass tank, right in the middle of a table, was a big, fat frog.

Betsan!

Sadly, knowing that Gwydion's friend was lost forever unless Gwydion could organise a rescue before the witch decided to mix bits of Betsan into a spell, Bugsy and Fang began the long journey back to Castell Du.

But although Fang had followed Betsan's trail *to* the cottage, he hadn't thought of checking to see if she had gone *away* from the cottage, too.

Which only goes to prove that both dogs and dragons can be fooled by witches, because we know perfectly well that Betsan got away, don't we?

Don't we?

CHAPTER SEVEN

Well, did she?

Of course she did. Mind, it was a bit hairy for a while, because running through a dark forest in the middle of the night with an evil witch chasing you is not a lot of fun. Betsan took off like a bat out of hell, even though she was wearing wellies, hoping she wouldn't bash into a tree in the darkness and knock herself unconscious. Fortunately, the wood was on her side (of course woods can be on a person's side: this is Ynys Haf, remember?) because the witch had a nasty habit of ripping branches off its trees to keep her fire going. I'm sure you already know that no reasonable wood minds a person helping herself to the bits of dead branch and twig that have already dropped off trees in the usual way. But ripping living branches off trees hurts them, and spoils the appearance of a tree, and after it's gone to all that trouble to grow into a nice tree-shape, too.

So if there was any danger of Betsan colliding with a trunk or a low branch, the tree rapidly bent sideways or up, so that she got through unscratched, unpoked and unbashed. While Betsan was making her getaway, the Witch was trying to start up her broomstick.

Normally, a witch's broomstick just zooms obediently away as soon as the witch hops aboard, and that would have been the end of Betsan, because she'd have been caught in a twinkle of a toad's eyeball. But this broomstick was made of a branch that the Witch had ripped off a tree, and it hadn't forgiven her. It quite often got its own back by tipping her into a pond, or flying her very close to swarms of hornets, or dumping her in a dollop of cow-poo. This time, the broomstick had been in the cottage minding its own business and had heard everything that had been going on – and being family, so to speak, of the wood, it also knew everything that was going on outside it. So of course it, too, was on Betsan's side, and it quite simply refused to start until it was certain that Betsan was far enough away to be safe from the witch.

So yes, Betsan got away, but she still had to find somewhere safe to sleep until it was light enough to continue her search for Gwydion. She'd learned her lesson (she thought). She wouldn't approach anyone else unless she *knew* they were goodies.

But in Ynys Haf, how could a mortal person tell?

In the meantime, however, the wood was still looking after her. It made itself a little path and guided Betsan's feet on to it. And when Betsan came to the end of the little path she found a small, dry cave just big enough for her, with an inviting pile of soft dead leaves and bracken that the wood had arranged for her. She was so tired that she didn't even wonder about that, or why the inside of the cave was light enough for her to see and not be afraid of the dark, but of course the wood had organised that, too. Grateful to be alive and not bubbling in a cauldron, Betsan slept soundly.

She woke to the sound of birdsong, and when she stepped outside the cave, stretching and yawning, she was amazed to see a bush filled with ripe blackberries. There was also a large patch of plump wild strawberries,

43

a hazelnut tree groaning with glossy brown nuts, with shells thin enough to crack in her fingers, all growing just outside the cave entrance. Best of all, there was a clear, sparkling spring bubbling with refreshing water!

She was amazed, because all those things arrive in totally different seasons – but you won't be, of course, because this is Ynys Haf, right?

When she had eaten (and she'd never, ever tasted fruit as good at that before, not even the magic raspberries from Gwydion's Flying Wand adventure) she made sure she hadn't left anything untidy lying about, like piles of nutshells, and set off in the direction that the sun was rising. She didn't exactly know why, but heading for the sun seemed like a good idea.

The wood was quite sad when she left: it didn't get many visitors who were as grateful as Betsan had been, or who left their wood so perfectly unharmed, and who left such a pleasant feeling behind her.

The edge of the wood was on a small rise, and when Betsan reached the top of it, she saw down below her the sea, sapphire, deep green, emerald, stretching forever, and a beach with small waves lapping at the shore. When she reached the edge of the sea, she took off her wellies and had a paddle. Wellies aren't made for hiking, and because the day was warm her feet were hot and achy. Wavelets trickled over her toes and cooled her, and she could have stayed there all day, except that she really wanted to go home. Mam would be horribly worried now that she'd been out all night, and there would be terrible trouble when she finally got back.

The thought of home made Betsan's eyes water, and

44

her lip trembled a bit, but she wasn't crying. *No point in crying*, she thought, sniffing. *Won't change anything. Besides, only wimps cry. I got myself into this, I'm jolly well going to get myself out.*

She turned to leave the beach, and for the first time, noticed a large cave. An old man stood in the entrance, watching her. He was tall and thin, and bony ankles and bare, knobbly feet stuck out from beneath a stained white robe. He wasn't a very clean looking old man, Betsan thought. He had a straggly, greyish beard and his long, greasy hair looked as if birds had been nesting in it. He must have been watching her the whole time she'd been on the beach.

While she decided what to do, she stopped and put her socks and wellies on, dusting sand from the soles of her feet so that she wouldn't get blisters. She sat on the sand and kept one eye on the old man, ready to run, wellies or not, if he approached her. The trouble was, she had to get past him to get off the seashore.

When she was ready, she set off, and as she drew close to him she nodded and smiled, politely. 'Good morning,' she said. 'What a lovely day!'

The old man scowled. 'You might think so,' he replied, 'but I don't.'

'Oh,' Betsan said, not quite sure what else to say.

'I don't suppose you've got a sausage about your person, have you?' he asked. 'I could murder a nice, golden brown pork sausage. With onions. I haven't had a sausage for centuries.'

Betsan shook her head. 'I haven't got any food, I'm afraid. But there's a wood a little way away, and there are all sorts of berries and nuts there if you're hungry.'

45

'Hungry? Of course I'm hungry! I've been stuck on this beach for the best part of three hundred and seventy-four years! And if you'd been stuck here for three hundred and seventy-four years with nothing but seagulls' eggs, roast puffin and winkles to eat, you'd fancy a pork sausage, too.'

'I expect I would.' Betsan tried to edge past the old man to get to the cliff path, but he blocked her way.

'If you haven't got a sausage, what about a nice bit of bacon?' he asked.

'Sorry, no bacon, either. If you don't like the food, why don't you leave the beach? Go and get something else to eat.'

The old man's watery eyes narrowed. 'Oh, you'd like that, wouldn't you? Did that Merlin send you? Try to tempt me off my beach with blandishments? Did he tell you to offer me sausage and bacon? Did he? Did he?'

'No! No one sent me. And I didn't say anything about sausages, you did.'

'But I bet you know perfectly well that if I leave this beach, Merlin can zap me, rightaway? Turn me into Druid Soup if he wants to!'

'Oh!' Betsan was unsure what else to say. 'No, I didn't know. I'm sorry.' Then something clicked in her brain. 'Did you say Merlin?' She knew that Merlin was Gwydion's Master, and if she could find Merlin, then Gwydion probably wouldn't be far behind.

'Yes, Merlin, Merlin, Merlin. That's all I ever hear, Merlin. He thinks he's so smart. He may have got the better of me once, but I'll make sure he doesn't do it again. If only I could get off this beach.'

He was still blocking her way. 'Why don't you just leave?' Betsan asked. 'No one's stopping you, as far as I can see?'

Suddenly the old man's expression changed. It stopped being cross and started to be friendly. Well, sort of. If you could call a smile that couldn't quite be called a smile, more just a set of (horribly black and rotten) teeth being bared, friendly. His attempts to look pleasant worried her more than his bad temper.

'You're quite right, nice, kind, sweet little girl,' he said, still smiling the awful, artificial smile. 'That's what I'll do. I'll leave. Right away. But it takes a very special person to help me, and I just know you are that person. You have a kind face. A sweet face. A dear little girl's sort of face.'

Yuk! Betsan thought. *He makes me want to bite him!* 'I'm not sure how I can help you.'

'Oh, it's the easiest thing in the world, dearie! The rules that silly old Merlin put on me – always joking, that Merlin, always joking! – say that I have to be invited to leave. Some stranger to Ynys Haf has to come and say, "Great Druid, I invite you to leave this place, forthwith and immediately". Then I can get away. Only strangers don't come to Ynys Haf very often. And now you have! A perfect stranger in more ways than one. *Isn't* life remarkable?'

Betsan considered. She certainly was a stranger, no doubt about that. If she invited the old man to leave, perhaps she could make a bargain. He could tell her how to find Merlin, and she could help him off the beach. Well, it was worth a try.

'Just supposing,' she began, 'just supposing I were

47

to say "Great Druid, I –' she stopped. She didn't want to say it in case the effect was immediate and she ended up helping him and he got away without helping her in return – 'what you said,' she amended, 'and got you off the beach, would you help me find Merlin?'

The Great Druid's eyes glittered. 'Of course I would, my dear. Just say the word and we'll help each other. Go on. You know you want to. Say the word, there's a dear. Then it's sausages for me! Oooh, sausages! And I'll fix that Merlin once and for all, I'll – ' He must have seen the doubtful look on Betsan's face. 'I'll pull his naughty old leg, I will!' he finished up, smiling that artificial smile.

Betsan sighed, hoping she was making the right decision. 'Great Druid, I invite you to leave this place, forthwith and immediately.'

For a few seconds, nothing happened. Then the Great Druid picked up the hem of his grimy robe (which Betsan saw was covered in bird droppings and egg-stains) and danced a jig, his pale, hairy ankles flashing in the sunlight. He twirled round and round and round.

'Gotcha!' he shouted, and disappeared in a puff of smoke.

'You rotten cheat!' Betsan yelled. 'You promised!'

But Betsan was used to looking on the bright side. At least she could get off the beach now the Great Druid wasn't standing in her way. She trudged to the top of the path and looked around her.

The trouble was, she didn't have a clue which way to go, except she didn't want to go back the way she'd come. She couldn't risk running into that witch again!

So, tying the sleeves of her waterproof jacket more tightly round her middle, she set off inland, away from the wood.

She hadn't gone very far when she got that *'someone's watching me!'* feeling again . . .

CHAPTER EIGHT

Bugsy and Fang scurried back to Castell Du. Bugsy flew in through Merlin's turret window, while Fang hurtled up the stairs three at a time, and by the time he got to the top he was horribly dizzy. He had terrible trouble with spiral staircases, and Merlin's tower had about seven hundred steps. He'd tried to count them once, and had needed to lie down afterwards in a dark room, until he stopped feeling sick. Going round and round and counting at the same time wasn't good for a dog.

All that could be seen of Gwydion was his tail end sticking out of the cupboard. Now, I expect you complain and look miserable when your Mum makes you tidy your room (go on, I bet it's untidy right now!) so I expect you'll feel sympathetic towards Gwydion, because Magic Cupboards are even worse than your wardrobe and chest-of-drawers. Magic Cupboards go back for miles, and Gwydion was only about a metre into it.

Bugsy took a closer look at Gwydion's finds. There were empty bottles, full bottles without labels, a tennis racket without any strings, a violin in the same condition, several skeletons of extinct creatures, a dinosaur egg and some jelly beans. Bugsy thought about eating the jelly beans, but on second thoughts decided not to risk it. Goodness knows how long they'd been there. Besides, they might be magical ones. There did seem to be an awful lot of green ones, which was usually a bad sign.

Bugsy perched on the curtain rail to finish off a chop bone he'd hidden there a while ago. When Fang had got his breath back and his head had stopped spinning, he went and attracted Gwydion's attention by putting his cold nose on Gwydion's hot back, just where his jerkin parted company with his breeches.

'Aaargh!' Gwydion jumped in shock, hit his head on a shelf and backed out into the room. A spider was building a web between the tuft of hair that stuck out on the crown of his head, and his left ear.

'Don't *do* that, Fang, you rotten dog!' Gwydion complained, shoving him away. 'Where have you been, anyway?'

'Greeaowr-uff!' Fang said, which meant, 'Tracking down Betsan for you, dummy!'

'I should think so,' Gwydion said, rubbing the dog's ears. 'You should apologise, too!'

Fang sighed. Honestly, was there any point at all in attempting to communicate with this idiot? He didn't understand a word, did he? And they said humans were intelligent!

He gave Bugsy a Look, and the dragon flew down. He perched on the cupboard door and blew a short lick of flame. Gwydion, alarmed, crawled backwards and scrambled to his feet.

'Cut that out, Bugsy! You know that's not allowed indoors!'

Bugsy delicately burped another short stream of flame. Gwydion backed away still more. Then Fang gently took Gwydion's hand between his jaws and tugged. Gwydion tried to remove his hand from a place that was both uncomfortably sharp and

51

disgustingly soggy, but Fang held on, and slowly, slowly, dragged Gwydion towards the tower door. He hoped the boy would get the idea before they reached the spiral stairs, because Fang found it hard enough going *up* the right way round. Going *down* backwards would be horrible.

Luckily, Gwydion did. 'Oh, I get it!' he said, his face lighting up, 'you want me to go with you, right? You want to show me something!'

'Rawwff!' Fang commented, which meant 'hoo-flipping-ray!'

'Well, good dog and all that, but I'm not allowed!' Gwydion said, relieved now that Fang had released his hand. 'Merlin will sprogfoddle me if I don't do my chores.'

Bugsy and Fang exchanged Looks again. Then, Fang and Bugsy both got behind Gwydion, Fang shoved the back of his knees and nipped his ankles, and Bugsy tried to scorch the back of his neck a little – all to encourage him ever so gently to GO DOWNSTAIRS.

Naturally, Gwydion went. While he clattered down the stairs trying to protect his neck, his knees and his ankles, he hoped he wouldn't meet his Master coming up. He wanted to be back inside the cupboard long before Merlin returned, and hoped no one would see him and tattle-tale. With luck, Merlin would be none the wiser.

At the foot of the tower he hid inside an arched doorway and peered out, making sure that no one could see him, then slipped silently across the drawbridge. The gatekeeper should have spotted him.

52

The gatekeeper should have been alert as a hawk and at his post and standing to attention and a lot of other things, but in fact he was flat on his back in a sunny corner of the battlements, dreaming he was at the Century Stadium. Wales was playing England at a jousting tournament, and Wales was winning, seventy-nine falls to two. The gatekeeper had a happy smile on his face, and every now and again his arms and legs twitched like a dog running in its dreams. He certainly didn't notice the three figures slipping across the drawbridge he was supposed to be guarding.

Safely away from the Castle, Gwydion followed Fang. The dog loped through the woods – this time going directly to the witch's cottage rather than all round the mountains and twice through the bog. Betsan needed rescuing, and she needed rescuing now.

On the edge of the wood, the big, dark dog paused, and pointed with his nose at the cottage nestling in the trees. For once in his life Gwydion understood immediately, and groaned.

'Oh, *no*! Don't say Blodwen Wartnose has got her?'

Fang and Bugsy, who had perched on Gwydion's shoulder, both nodded.

Gwydion sighed. 'Oh well, I suppose I'd better try to rescue her, hadn't I?'

They crept forward, hiding behind trees, bushes and boulders. They opened the garden gate, tiptoed up the path, and when they reached the cottage, Gwydion put his eye to the same knothole that Betsan had peeped through, and peered inside. The cottage appeared to be empty. To make sure, he went and peered through another knothole in the other shutter, and then through the letterbox. Despite her traditional witch appearance (hooked nose and pointy hat and all that) Blodwen Wartnose was a very modern sort of Old Hag. However, because no one had invented the Post Office yet, her letter box was both *very* up-to-date and *very* useless.

The cottage still looked empty, so Gwydion lifted the latch and slipped inside.

'Betsan,' he whispered loudly, 'Betsan, where are you?'

Fang went straight to the table with the large tank on it. It was a very nice tank, and there was a shallow tray of clean water for the frog to sit in, a rock for it to sit on, and from the little pile of fly-wings in the corner, plenty of insects to eat, supplied by the Witch. The frog, green, slimy and unblinking, sat in the middle of its pond. Bugsy perched on the edge of the tank, looking in, which made the frog very nervous. It sat very still and concentrated on pretending it wasn't there at all.

'Betsan?' Gwydion called, looking inside a chest.

'Betsan, are you there?' he whispered, looking into the larder.

'Betsan? It's OK, we've come to rescue you!' he said, peering inside the stove.

Bugsy took off from the tank, perched on Gwydion's head, and by digging his claws in very gently, managed to turn Gwydion's head round. He noticed Fang sitting patiently beside the frog's tank.

'Oh, crumbs!' he groaned. 'Don't say Blodwen Wartnose has already enchanted her! Oh, crumbs, she's a frog! I'll have to take her back to Merlin's

54

tower to change her back. I *think* I can do it. If I use
Merlin's spell book. Oh, Betsan,' he groaned, 'why
didn't you stay safely in your own Time?'

He had one hand groping inside the tank trying to
pick up the frog, when Blodwen Wartnose, who all
this time had been catching up on her beauty sleep up
on the sleeping platform, woke up. The beauty sleep
hadn't worked. She poked her ugly nose over the edge
and saw Gwydion.

'What are you doing in my house, Boy?' she
croaked (she was always croaky when she woke up, at
least until she'd had her cup of tea).

'Noth-noth-nothing,' Gwydion stammered, clutching
the slimy frog to his chest.

'What are you doing with my frog?' she demanded,
as Gwydion backed towards the door. 'Put it back at
once, do you hear?'

The witch was out of bed in a trice and clambering
down the ladder. Just before he turned and ran,
Gwydion noticed that under her black dress she wore
stripy purple knickers which reached almost to her
bony knees.

Flinging open the cottage door, Gwydion pounded
back down the garden path, past the clumps of deadly
nightshade, poisonous mushrooms, dandelion beds
and thistle bushes, out of the garden and into the
woods. The frog closed its eyes and wondered what
would happen to it. At least this person clutching him
didn't seem to be French, although being only a frog
he wasn't terribly sure what a French person looked
like. However, he had heard on the pondweed-vine
that French people *ate frogs' legs*. He shuddered in

horror and pictured all the legless frogs in French ponds. How could a frog hop without legs? Unless perhaps French frogs had extra ones, some to be eaten and some to hop with. All that thinking was hurting the frog's brain, and besides, his thoughts were scary, so he stopped thinking altogether. It was safer when he didn't think.

Fang overtook Gwydion (he wasn't at all keen on witches) and Bugsy fluttered overhead. Soon the three of them reached the trees, which of course were on their side against Blodwen Wartnose, so Gwydion didn't trip over roots and branches, Bugsy didn't fly into any trunks, and Fang concentrated very hard and tried not to smell the rabbits.

Blodwen Wartnose was trying to kick-start her broomstick. On the twenty-fourth try, by which time Blodwen was red in the face, very cross and rather sweaty (yes, I know ladies don't sweat, they perspire, but I never said Blodwen was a lady, did I?). At the twenty-fourth try the broomstick took off, flew half a mile in a very looping, upsy, downsy way, which made her feel airsick, flew upside down for exactly a mile and a quarter, then zoomed earthwards at about warp speed nine, depositing Blodwen into a bramble bush.

'You useless heap of junk, you!' she screamed, removing herself painfully from the thorns. 'I'm going to chop you up for firewood!'

You'll have to catch me first, the broomstick thought. It went back to the wood, found the tree it had been ripped from, and settled in the branches. From that day, there wasn't a piece of wood in Ynys Haf that was prepared to co-operate with Blodwen

Wartnose, so she had to buy a bike. But that's another story.

Meanwhile, Gwydion, still clutching the frog, ran back to Merlin's tower, trying all the way to remember the spell for turning people who had been changed into frogs back into people again. He thought that there was Rampion in it, or was it Devilsbit Scabious?

CHAPTER NINE

Betsan was right: someone *was* watching her. Lots of someones, actually. Even though her wellies were getting very uncomfortable, and she was so hot in her denim jeans that she thought she might possibly melt, she hardly noticed because she had this weird feeling that every step she took, eyes were upon her.

Several times she turned, quickly, hoping to catch the watcher, but each time she swung round no one was there. At first, she felt scared, but by the time she'd walked for about an hour, the feeling was so strong that she was beginning to get angry. How dare people watch her and not show themselves? How dare they spy on her? Eventually she found a shady tree, sat down beneath it, folded her arms and said to the empty air, 'I'm absolutely fed up with being spied on. I'm not going a step further unless you show yourself.'

There was a sudden silence. A real silence: no buzzing bees, no birdsong, no chirping insects, nothing except absolute soundlessness. And then a small, birdlike voice said, 'If we must show ourselves, then you must shut your eyes first.'

Ourselves? Betsan thought. How many ourselves were there, then? She looked about her, nervously. Suppose she shut her eyes and something terrible happened? Suppose a huge wolf with savage, humungous fangs leapt upon her while her eyes were shut? Suppose it was a whole horde of witches out for her blood? She chewed her lip and thought about it, and worried a lot – and then decided she might as well try, because she didn't want to carry on walking with this horrible feeling of someone spying on her. She stood up, in case she had to run very fast for any reason.

'All right then,' she agreed, 'but I'm *trusting* you, so no unkind tricks.' And she shut her eyes.

After a few seconds, the small, chirping voice spoke again. 'You may look, now,'

At first, Betsan couldn't see anything. It was a bit like – ooh, how can I describe it? Well, if you've ever picked runner beans from the garden, when you first look, there aren't any there, and then suddenly you see them, clusters of them, hidden by the green surrounding them. And there they were.

Dozens of tiny people, barely there people, gauzy people you could almost see through, they were so delicate. Small, pointed faces looked up at her, great, sky-coloured, liquid eyes watched her, fragile bodies perched on trees, lay on the grass at her feet, fluttered on filmy wings almost within reach.

'You're Tylwyth Teg!' she breathed. 'Real fairies.'

'I told you she would see us, Arian,' one of them twittered, smiling.

'But she's mortal, Aur,' the other, a small tawny-haired fairy complained. 'Mortals shouldn't ever feel us around them, and they only see us if we want them to.'

'If she's here in Ynys Haf then she's a special mortal,' a third said, flying close to Betsan's face, delicate wings fanning Betsan's hair. 'She must certainly have met magic in her world.'

'I have, I have,' Betsan said delightedly. 'I met

59

Gwydion, and I'm trying to find him so that I can go home. Can you help me, please?'

'Does she mean Gwydion Dragonson? Do you mean Gwydion Dragonson, mortal?'

'I don't know. I know his name is Gwydion, but I don't exactly know his surname. But his Master is Merlin the Magician.'

'Merlin? Great Merlin? Then he is Gwydion Dragonson for certain.'

'Oh,' Betsan said, 'that's nice. But please, can you help me find him?'

'Can we –'

'– help her?'

'– find Gwydion –'

'– Dragonson?'

'Do we want to –'

' – help her?' several voices said at once.

'Shall we –'

' – be kind –'

'– or unkind?'

'Unkind is fun, but –'

'Oh, please?' Betsan begged. 'My Mam is going to be so worried about me. I've just got to get back.'

The Tylwyth Teg went into an airborne huddle. The one named Arian seemed to be the leader.

'We'll help you,' she said at last, 'but you must give us something in return. What shall it be, sisters?'

'She must tell us some stories,' Aur said, folding her arms. 'Stories first, help after.'

Arian nodded her agreement. 'Can you tell stories, mortal?'

Betsan nodded. Of course she could tell stories! She

had loads and loads filed away in her head, the ones that Mam and Dad had told her when she was small. 'I know *millions* of stories!' she boasted.

(Now this was Betsan's Big Mistake. Fairies are very literal people. That means that they take you at your very word. If you were to say "I'm so hungry I could eat a horse," they would bring you a live one, and wait for you to do it . . .)

'Would you like to hear *Sleeping Beauty*?' Betsan asked. The little people whizzed around excitedly, the wind from their wings making Betsan's hair whip into her face.

'Tell us, tell us,' they begged.

'You must come with us,' Arian demanded, and Betsan, surrounded by small, persistent winged creatures, was escorted down the hill and into the darkness of a cave. She was a bit nervous at first, because it was pitch dark inside, but then a door was flung open and she gasped at the brightness. Lights and mirrors and glinting gold and flashing diamonds were everywhere, and more and more of the tiny people gathered round at the sight of a mortal in their midst. They tugged Betsan to a golden chair, and when she was sitting, they clustered round to listen.

'Once upon a time, in a far-off land,' Betsan began, and the Tylwyth Teg gave a great, collective sigh of delight as they settled to listen. When *Sleeping Beauty* was over, Betsan told them *Red Riding Hood*, and *Twm Siôn Cati*, and *Siôn and the Bargain Bee*, and then she told them as much as she could remember of *Stig of the Dump* and then began the story of *Branwen*, and *Jack and the Beanstalk*. She told stories until she was hoarse, and still the little people clamoured for more.

So she told them *The Owl who was Afraid of the Dark*, and *The Caterpillar that Couldn't*, the legends from *The Back End of Nowhere,* and *The Princess and the Pea* (they liked that one), and then she begged for a rest.

'No! More stories, more stories,' they begged, and so Betsan went on and on, until her voice was almost gone.

'I'm sorry,' she croaked, 'but I've got to have a rest, honestly. I'm exhausted. I'm hoarse as a horse, honest I am.' She hoped the joke might make them pity her a bit.

'You'll tell us more tomorrow,' Arian said, scowling, and the others clapped their hands and nodded.

'I was rather hoping you might help me find Gwydion tomorrow,' Betsan said. 'I've kept my part of the bargain, haven't I?'

'No you haven't, not at all,' Arian said angrily. 'You've only just begun. You said you knew a million stories, and you've only told us thirteen little ones. Before we help you, you must tell us *all* your million stories! That was the bargain, mortal!'

'What?' Betsan's jaw dropped. She didn't know a million stories, no one did! She'd been exaggerating, that's all. It was a whatchamacallit – a figure of speech. Besides, if she was stuck there for the length of time it would take to tell a million stories, she'd be there until she was an old, old lady – forever, maybe. 'I don't really know a million stories!' she said apologetically. 'That was just a sort of a saying. I'm sorry.'

'You're sorry?' Arian shrieked, her pointed face suddenly ugly. 'You lied, mortal. You promised! People who lie and break their promises must be punished!'

'Punish her, punish her!' all the Tylwyth Teg shrieked, and Betsan covered her ears with her hands as the tiny creatures flew at her, beating her face with their wings. She crouched down in a huddle, put her arms over her head to shield it, and stayed there until they stopped. She stayed, crouched for several minutes after the attack seemed to have ended. Then she edged one eye open and peered over her sheltering arm. They'd gone. She was all alone in the beautiful, glowing chamber. Cautiously, she got up. They were really gone, all of them, and the doorway out of the chamber and into the cave was just over there . . .

But when she tried to move towards the door, she couldn't. She couldn't walk. It felt as if she was trying to wade through waist-deep treacle. She tried to crawl, but that didn't work, either. Wildly, she looked around her: there was another door in the far corner, and when she tried to go in that direction, it was easy, nothing held her back.

Of course, she should have realised that if magic allowed her to go there when it wouldn't let her go in the other direction, then that way wasn't likely to be an escape route, was it? But Betsan was so tired from storytelling, and so frightened at being trapped once again, and so afraid that the Tylwyth Teg might come back and make her tell more stories, that she wasn't thinking straight, so she went through the doorway anyway.

She found herself in a narrow passageway. Roots twisted overhead to make the ceiling, and the ground was made of trodden earth. Eventually she came to a place where there were three doors. Cautiously, she opened the first, peered out then decided to take that path, closing the door behind her. She followed the passage round to the left, where the ground seemed to rise slightly. She hoped it might lead to the outside. Eventually she came to a place where there were three more doors. This time she opened the second door and went through. Roots twisted over her head, and the ground was made of trodden earth. It was another passageway, exactly like the first – or perhaps it was the first, and she was going round in circles. This time, she turned to the right . . .

But several more doors, several more tunnels and several hours later . . .

Betsan knew that she was totally, utterly, completely lost.

CHAPTER TEN

It wasn't Devilsbit Scabious. It wasn't Rampion. It wasn't even castor oil and custard. It wasn't anything at all of the two thousand and one different ingredients and spells that Gwydion tried. (And that was a 'figure of speech', too, just like Betsan's 'million stories'. He really only tried eight hundred and seventy-two.)

Whatever he did, however, the frog just sat froggily on the table in Gwydion's chamber. It looked, and was, very, very bored. It doesn't take much to amuse a frog: a nice bit of muddy pond, a reasonably attractive lady frog, a bit of pondweed for decoration, a good supply of mayflies and stuff, and your average frog is happy. But this frog had none of these and it was bored, hungry and fed up. And nervous, because there was a large brownish-black creature staring at it from a distance of about six inches (frogs don't do metric measurements, I'm afraid) and a small red, scaly dragon sitting on a curtain rail munching on a bone. When it burped, it burped fire, and frogs don't much like fire. It ruins their complexions.

Gwydion ran his fingers through his hair, which dislodged the spider but didn't do much else for it, because his hands were covered in honey (the honey, cat's-ear and toadflax spell). On his nose was a dab of very expensive shrew oil (Don't ask where *that* comes from. You don't want to know). Strewn all round him were bits of herbs, exotic spices, elephant hair, crocodile eyelashes (very rare) and rather a lot of mouse-droppings, because Bugsy had managed to upset the cage and all the mice had escaped, except the one he frizzled accidentally. He ate it though, so it wasn't wasted.

Gwydion couldn't think of any more spells. He'd tried every single spell in the book, and still the frog sat there, and not Betsan.

Merlin would be back soon, and he hadn't finished the cupboard, let alone any of the other tasks he'd been set. Merlin was going to be so mad at him he might turn Gwydion into a frog, and then there'd be two of them. At least then Betsan would have someone to talk to.

'Oh, Bendigeidfran's bellybutton, Betsan, why didn't you stay in your own Time?' he said exasperatedly.

Fang gazed at him in disgust. Surely he wasn't giving up already? He hadn't even tried Merlin's magic stick yet!

There was a good reason why Gwydion hadn't tried the wand. Last time he'd borrowed it, Merlin had said quite firmly that if he ever found Gwydion anywhere near it again, he would do something to him so terrible that it would take approximately a thousand years for assorted bits of Gwydion to stop stinging. *And then it would start to really hurt!*

Now, if you'd been Gwydion, would you have risked it? No, neither would I.

But, there was Betsan, as frogged as a frog can be. There was just one measly, tatty, ancient spell book left to try. Sighing, his head aching, Gwydion picked up the book and began to read. Suddenly, he sat up. This was it! It had to be!

66

Ye Spelle (it said) *forre to remoove inchantryments From Thynges That Has been Whoolly Enchanterated into Other Thynges and What the Master Wyshes to Chaynge Backe Forthewithe*

The old spellwriter couldn't spell, (neither could Gwydion) but this had to be the right spell. Even the ingredients sounded right:

Unikornes Horne, Dryed Toade Spawne.

Gwydion turned the page to see the rest of the ingredients, and ran his finger down the list. He had them all, even the raspberries. He fetched a bowl and began to chuck stuff in, then from a big flask he sploshed in some distilled water and mixed. At last, carefully, he upended the bowl over the frog's head. Gwydion crossed his fingers, his eyes, his legs and arms and hoped. Then, he lifted the bowl. Underneath was –

The frog.

'Aaaargh!' Gwydion howled. 'I did every mud-sucking, belly-belching, worm-scrambling, newt-knotting thing exactly right! Why hasn't it worked? What is wrong with you, frog? Why are you doing this to me? Why, why, why, why, why?' And lots more like that, which did absolutely no good at all because the frog wasn't paying any attention. It had uncurled its long tongue and taken a lick of the stuff in the bowl. It was so good, it had some more. The reason the frog was enjoying it so much was (a) he was hungry, (b) it was there, and (c) Gwydion had turned over two pages at once and most of the spell he'd used was actually a recipe for Summer Pudding (Ynys Haf style).

And then, while Gwydion was in mid-tantrum and the frog was in mid-slurp, Merlin came back. Neither of them heard him coming, but Fang and Bugsy did, because dogs and dragons have the sort of ears that can hear magic.

Merlin appeared from the feet up: first a pair of trainers, then a pair of denim jeans and a black T-shirt with some silver stars and 'MAGIC MUSIC – MERLIN AND TALIESIN, WORLD TOUR 2072' on it. Above that was a face with a rather sunburned nose, little round sunglasses, and a baseball cap on sideways (magicians never wear them forward or backward, always sideways). The face was quite a young face: if you met him, you would think he was about as old as your Dad, or maybe your favourite uncle. Merlin might be several hundred centuries old, but he certainly didn't look it – when he didn't want to. He only ever wore his long robes and white beard when he wanted to impress people, or was having lunch with the Dragonking, who liked his Magician to look like a Magician occasionally.

He stood silently behind Gwydion for a while, watching his apprentice rant and rave and throw a really spectacular temper fit. Bugsy shot straight through the window and Fang disappeared under the bed. Only the frog and Gwydion were completely unaware that the Master had arrived.

At last, by the time Gwydion had bent double on his knees so that his forehead was resting on the floor and his fists were hammering on it, Merlin reached out a foot and prodded him.

Gwydion went very still. He didn't look round. He

knew exactly who it was. After a ve-e-e-ery lo-o-o-o-ong while he plucked up courage and peeped up, under his own armpit, just to check.

'Mer-mer-merlin?' he said, just to make absolutely sure that he wasn't having a nightmare.

Unfortunately, he wasn't. The nightmare was all too real.

Merlin frowned. When Merlin frowned, the sun went in, thunderclouds formed, and lightning got all ready to zap and fork and sizzle. 'Who else?'

Gwydion wondered what might be the best thing to do. Crawl for the door? Roll onto his back, close his eyes and pretend he'd fainted? Pretend he was looking for something valuable that had accidentally rolled out of the cupboard in Merlin's tower, down three flights of spiral stairs, round three corners, through four doors, and under the table in his chamber?

Too late. Merlin picked him up by the scruff of his neck until Gwydion was nose-to-nose with him.

'Why,' he enquired, in a dangerously quiet sort of voice, 'are you here and not head down in the store-cupboard?'

'I, I, I –' Gwydion began.

'Don't interrupt, boy. Why is there a frog on your table, hmmm? A frog covered in –' he reached out a finger on his spare hand, dipped it in the mixture in the bowl and tasted. '– Summer Pudding?'

'I, I, I –' Gwydion tried again.

'I said, don't interrupt. Why are ALL my spell books lying around on the floor of your room? Why are a lot of my most expensive ingredients scattered all over the place? If you wish to enjoy any more birthdays, boy, you'd better have a *really, really good explanation!'*

Gwydion thought about pretending he'd had a brainstorm and gone mad. He thought about pretending he was someone else in Gwydion's skin. He considered telling Merlin that two or three hundred ruthless, fierce robbers had invaded the tower and despite a brave but useless battle on Gwydion's part, had torn the tower apart in their fury. Then he decided it was probably easier (and safer) to tell the truth.

'It's all to do with the time your wand disappeared, Merlin,' he began miserably. 'It's a long story.'

Merlin dropped him onto the bed. Clouds of dust shot out, and Gwydion sneezed. 'Bless you,' Merlin said, but not as if he meant it particularly kindly. 'I have all the Time in the world, boy. Speak.'

So Gwydion did.

'And that's why the frog is covered in Summer Pudding,' he finished sadly. 'I tried everything.'

'I hope you didn't try my wand?' Merlin said fiercely, his nose about an inch away from Gwydion's.

'N-n-no, Sir,' Gwydion said.

'Then let's try it now,' Merlin said unexpectedly, and waved his right hand over his head. The wand instantly appeared in it, and Merlin tapped the frog on the head with it, just to get its attention.

'*Elmiogorious rana temporaria, transformicariolatus humanicus feminaria,'* he boomed, and flourished the wand three times over the steadily licking frog, who ignored him completely. There was a very small explosion, barely enough to

70

scatter a ripe dandelion clock, a puff of smoke that completely concealed the frog, and when it cleared there was –

A frog.

Merlin frowned and removed his sunglasses. 'That's odd,' he said, bending his long body to look closely at the creature. He put down his wand and picked up the frog. He held the frog on the palm of his hand and looked closely into its eyes. The frog stared back. It couldn't move or even blink: it was too full of Summer Pudding.

'Gwydion, you idiot, you know what this is?'

Gwydion shook his head. 'No, Master. What is it?'

'It's a frog, you clown. It certainly isn't some little human that's trespassing in Ynys Haf, that's certain.'

'But it must be!' Gwydion wailed. 'It was on Blodwen Wartnose's table! What else can it be?'

'Well, if it was on Blodwen's table it was probably *about* to be frog omelette,' Merlin said. 'Turn the poor creature loose and we'll see what we can see.'

So Gwydion released the frog into the pond where it spent the rest of its life boring its froggy friends with tales of its adventures. Gwydion turned and climbed the stairs to Merlin's tower.

Inside was Merlin's magic mirror.

CHAPTER ELEVEN

Meanwhile, Betsan was sitting miserably on the earthen floor of the passageway. She was exhausted, hungry and fed up. She was also very cross.

Cross at herself for getting into this mess in the first place even though Gwydion had warned her, and cross at the Tylwyth Teg for not knowing that 'a million stories' didn't actually *mean* a million. She was also cross at this stupid place for having no way out, cross at Gwydion for starting the whole thing off by coming into her Time, cross at her Mam for not being around when she was needed. She probably would have been cross at the Welsh Assembly, Scott Quinnell and all of the Stereophonics, too, except she couldn't think of anything to blame them for.

She wished for fish and chips. She wished for a nice, hot shower. She wished for a big carton of ice-cold orange juice, and she wished for home and bed. But, even though Ynys Haf is magic through and through, she didn't get any of it. What she got was a mole.

First there was a disturbance in the earth at her feet, then there was a small hill. Shortly after that, a little pink bewhiskered nose followed by a small velvety head appeared, and then two strong, spadelike paws. Betsan had never seen a mole up close, although she'd heard Granch complain about the mess they made of his lawn. It was rather sweet.

'Hello, little furry chum!' she whispered softly, not to scare it away. She was delighted to have some company.

'What?' the mole snapped. 'Who's that? What do you want? I'm not anybody's little furry chum, least of all yours. Why are you botherising me? Scram. Hop it. Go away. Who do you think you are, anyway, talking to me?'

Betsan was so taken aback by the creature's rudeness that she didn't stop to wonder that it could talk.

'It's me talking to you,' she snapped back, 'Betsan Price from Blaengwynfi, and I can't go away, I'm stuck here, and anyway I've probably got as much right here as you have, so there.'

'You haven't either. You've no business being here at all. You're not one of those wretched little waftsome, wraithsome creatures that flit around confusticating people, are you? They make me so cross I want to reach for my fly-swatter to splat them, they do.'

'If you mean the Tylwyth Teg, no I'm not. I'm their prisoner.'

The mole glared at her. 'Are you now? And how did you get your stupid self into *that* sort of predicklement? But if it's a long story, don't bother to tell me. I'm a busy mole. I'm in far too much of a hurry to listen to long stories.'

'It *is* a long story, so I suppose you'd better buzz off. You might as well anyway, you're so horrible. I never knew moles were such grouches!'

'I'm allowed! Moles are famous for their bad tempers. We're very stressed, us moles, very stressed. There's always a tunnel to be dug, worms to be whiffled, slugs to be slurped. So get out of my way and let me get on with it, you great big ugglesome, clumsy, horrendible creature.'

It was altogether too much. Betsan grabbed the mole round its portly middle just before it disappeared, and hauled it out of the earth. She held it, squirming wildly, at eyeball level and glared at it.

'I'm not a big ugglesome creature, I'm a person in trouble. And it's you who's horrendible, not me. I'd help *you* if *you* were in trouble, but all you can think of is worms and slugs and tunnels and not helping at all. You're useless. You should be ashamed of yourself, being so horrible to someone in trouble.' And she put the mole back on the ground beside its hole.

Surprisingly, the mole didn't dive headfirst in and make its escape. It stood there, gazing up at Betsan. It seemed to be trying to look guilty. After a while, it crawled onto her jeans leg and looked up. 'I'm not useless,' it said. 'I'm not horrendible. I just have difficulty with being friendly; it's my nature. And all the pressure and stress, of course. But I can help you, if you are brave enough.'

'Oh, I can be brave,' Betsan said hopefully. 'Betsan the Brave, that's me. But how can you help me? Not meaning to be unkind, but you aren't very big, are you?'

'Don't go away,' the mole replied, and disappeared into its hole. A little time later the earth all round Betsan began to erupt with molehills. Dozens of them, and soon each hill was crowned by a velvety head and thrusting, digging paws.

And shortly after that, the ground collapsed.

Betsan shot downward in a flurry of earth, wanting

to shriek but afraid to open her mouth in case it was filled with earth or worse. Down and down she fell, feet first, rushing through terrifying blackness until she landed with a thump on a heap of dead leaves in a place that had at least a little light.

She looked around her. The walls were rock, and the roof was arched and high. It seemed to be a cave. What light there was came from a hole in the roof far above, and in the opposite corner to the place she'd come through, there was a large opening in the rocky wall. The mole arrived beside her, puffing and out of breath.

'That wasn't so scary!' Betsan said. 'Is that the way out?' She pointed to the opening.

'The scary bit is still to come, human,' the mole said. 'That's the way out, it's true, but it's a long, long way, and it's twistsome-turnsome and very dark. I will help you, but you must do as I say without questioning. And if it should come back, I will run. I'm terrible afeared of it.'

'It?' Betsan said suspiciously, 'what do you mean "it"?'

'A great, big, hugesome beast with red jaws and sharp teeth,' the mole said, shutting its eyes tightly, 'a hugesome, huffsome beast that roars like thunder. It has wings and talons and mighty scales that the sharpest sword can't penetrate. It eats many molefolk.'

'But not people, right?' Betsan asked nervously.

'Oh, it eats people, too,' the mole replied, opening its eyes. 'When it can lay fangs on them. It's very fond of people, it is. It much prefers people to moles.'

'So where is it?' Betsan whispered.

75

'It's fooding-time for the Creature. The greatsome gibbous moon is aloft and alight and the Creature will be hunting.'

'So we'd better get moving, right?' Betsan said. 'Quick.'

Betsan followed the mole into the tunnel. Within seconds the tiny creature was lost from view in the darkness. Betsan walked, her hands outstretched in front of her, feeling very frightened and blind as a – as a mole, she thought. It was so dark that it was like having a big, black blanket over her head. It was so dark that she had difficulty breathing.

'Mole, are you there? Mole?'

A small voice came from by her feet. 'Of course I am. Where else would I be?'

'Would it be a good idea if we kept talking so that we don't lose sight of each other?'

'I won't lose sight of you. I see best in the dark.'

'Oh.'

'But if you would like to sing, I would like to hear you.'

So Betsan sang.

She sang *Ten Green Bottles,* and *The Ash Grove,* and *Dafydd y Garreg Wen*, and just about every other song she could think of. Her voice was already hoarse from storytelling, but still she sang. Hearing her voice in the absolute, blanketing darkness seemed to help.

And then, there was another sound. It was like a strong wind howling in a chimney, but the breeze was hot and smelled, Betsan decided, rather like someone who needed to brush their teeth more often.

After the howling wind-sound, there was a rustling,

scraping sound, like someone dragging a large dustbin across gravel. A dustbin the size of a double-decker bus . . .

After that, there was a hiccup. Not a human-sized hiccup, though, but one that could only have come from something very, extraordinarily, amazingly large.

'Um, mole?'

'Be quiet!' the mole said in the tiniest possible whisper. 'Don't move or speak if you want to breathe any more, ever!'

Betsan backed against the tunnel wall and froze. She held her breath, and she could hear the blood whooshing round her body, and her heart thumping, and her stomach rumbling (well, she was scared *and* hungry).

Whatever it was, was coming closer. The dustbin-on-gravel sound was getting louder and louder, and the huffing and hiccuping were getting louder and louder, and Betsan shut her eyes and wished with all her might that she was somewhere else. She felt a tiny, barely-there weight on her wellie, and then an even tinier voice said,

'It is the Dragonbeast. If it smells you, you are dead. Unless it has already killed and eaten.'

And then the Dragonbeast was there. It almost filled the entire tunnel. She couldn't see it, but she heard its harsh breathing, and the scrape, scrape of its wings and talons on the tunnel walls and floor.

And then something huge was sniffing at her. There was a terrible temptation to put out her hand and shove it away, but she squinched her eyes and kept as still as she could. She clenched her fists and held her breath and wondered if she'd be able to tell Maldwyn about meeting her first dragon or if her last moment had come and she wouldn't be able to tell him anything, ever again. Then, at last, it was moving away, past her, into the cave that was its lair. The dragging, scraping, gravelly sound seemed to go on forever.

Suddenly a loop of scaly tail whipped round her ankles and she was dragged off her feet, dragged back along the tunnel, while she flailed at walls and tried to hang on to bits of rock that weren't there. Then, just as it seemed she would be dragged back into the dragon's lair, the rough coil around her ankle loosed, and she was free. Betsan scrambled to her feet, sobbing with fear, and ran blindly back up the tunnel, crashing and blundering, her shins stinging where the scales had dragged skin off them. She ran until a stitch made her double up in pain and crouch, panting, in the darkness. But the dragon was gone and the tunnel was silent again except for her harsh, panicky breathing.

'That was a closesome thing,' the mole said in a normal voice. 'That was a most narrow escape, that was.'

Betsan's knees gave way and she slithered down the wall until she was sitting on the ground. 'You're telling me!' she said weakly.

'But you're safe, so no harm done,' the mole said matter-of-factly. 'Come on, come on, we haven't got all day.'

No harm done, except me nearly dying of fright, Betsan thought. And then they were outside again, in the moonlit night, and the air was fresh and clean and the musty, frowsty dragonsmell was completely gone.

Betsan filled her lungs over and over. *Ha!* she thought. *The Giant thought he had me. The Wild thought he had me. The Tylwyth Teg thought they had me. Well, they didn't, I got away! I even got away from a dragon without being eaten!*

'Thanks, mole,' she said. But the mole was gone, and only a fresh molehill showed that it had ever been there at all.

She hadn't gone more than a few steps away from the cave when she heard a low growl. It was a growl filled with such savagery that her blood, which had just defrosted itself and started circulating normally in her veins and arteries, froze all over again . . .

CHAPTER TWELVE

Merlin's big mirror was in the chamber at the very top of his tower. The tower was so high that if Gwydion looked out of the arrow-slit at the ground he always felt horribly dizzy. He didn't look out very often, because he wasn't allowed up there very often. It was Merlin's Special Room, and magician's apprentices weren't usually admitted.

The chamber was empty except for a huge, round table and a massive hourglass – like an oversized egg-timer – on a stand. Merlin turned it over and the sand began to trickle slowly through. On the table was something covered in a dark red cloth, and the same blood-coloured cloth was draped all round the walls, so that, Gwydion thought, if a person had a really good imagination, it was rather like being inside the big, red stomach of some terrifying beast.

Merlin whipped the cloth off the table, revealing the huge, ancient mirror. It was perfectly round, with an intricately carved wooden frame, and the glassy, mirror part of it was slightly curved like the mirrors in a fairground funhouse, so that when Gwydion looked in he appeared either short and fat like a dwarf, or tall and thin like a cameleopard. Or what he imagined a cameleopard might look like, because he'd never seen one.

Merlin bent over the mirror and huffed on the surface. Gwydion thought this might be part of the magic, but then Merlin used his sleeve to polish the bit he'd huffed on, so obviously it wasn't part of the magic, there was just a bit of a smear on it. Gwydion was quite keen to loiter at the edge of the room, but Merlin impatiently beckoned him forward.

'Come on, boy! You're the one who knows what this silly creature looks like. Describe her and I'll see if I can home in on her.'

Gwydion squinched up his eyes and tried to remember. 'Well, she's about my size, and she isn't fat and she isn't thin, and her hair is sort of medium brown, and it was long when I last saw her, and she ties it up behind her, only it won't be tied up right now because she lost the tie-thing, and her face has got spreckles on it, and she's friendly, and –'

Merlin was looking Exasperated. 'You've just described about ninety-eight per cent of the young female population of Ynys Haf, you utter idiot! What's special about her? There must be something! Come on, come on, I haven't got all day! I'm charging by the hour, you know. By the hour, and the sand is trickling through.'

'Charging for what?' Gwydion protested.

'Professional consultation!' Merlin replied loftily.

'But I haven't got any money!'

'You can pay me back in good behaviour.'

Gwydion chewed his fingernails and thought. 'I know,' he said at last, 'she's probably wearing trousers!'

'Well,' Merlin grumbled. 'At least that gives me a place to begin looking.' He bent over the mirror and waved his arms over the surface.

'Reflectoriatum, focusii questoratum,' he intoned, *'locatiaria feminarium* – er – wearing trousers,' he finished rather lamely.

81

Gwydion had a faint suspicion that all the magic was in the mirror and the wand, and the grand-sounding words didn't actually mean anything at all, that Merlin made them up as he went along to make his spells sound more impressive. But he wasn't going to say that. He valued his skin, and his shape, and his future.

The great mirror clouded and cleared. It was showing a picture of a small hut, and outside the hut was a small, red-haired, freckle-faced girl leading a goose on the end of a piece of string.

'Is that her?'

Gwydion shook his head. 'She doesn't have red hair, Master.'

'Why didn't you say so?'

Gwydion *was* going to point out that actually, he had, but he thought he'd better not.

Merlin waved his arms over the mirror to clear it. Two hours later (by the hourglass) after the mirror had found several dozen ten-year-old girls in Ynys Haf wearing trousers, Merlin was getting annoyed. Gwydion had had a good idea to narrow down the search quite a long time ago, but he was a bit afraid to suggest it. Merlin's temper was fraying a bit, he'd hurled his baseball cap at the wall half an hour ago, and his glasses had slithered down his nose. He glowered at Gwydion over the top of them.

'Are you sure she's here in Ynys Haf, boy?'

'Yessir. Sir, I, um –'

'Spit it out, boy!'

'Well, Master Merlin Sir, if you were to ask the mirror to show you ten-year-old, brown-haired, freckle-faced *lost* girls in trousers, might that help?'

Merlin glowered some more. 'It might. But I don't expect so. Far too simple.' Nevertheless he waved his arms over the mirror and bellowed,

'Feminarius perditorium brownus hairus
Ageum decalorium, freckledum facius.'

The mirror cleared, misted, cleared again – and there was Betsan!

'That's her!' Gwydion said excitedly. 'Where is she, Master? Can we go and find her now?'

'If that is *she*,' Merlin said, pompously correcting Gwydion's grammar, 'then her – I mean she – is in trouble.'

'She is?' Gwydion said anxiously, peering into the mirror.

'She is. For a start she's right on the edge of Tylwyth Teg country, and if they get hold of her, goodness knows how long it will take us to get her back. Also, she's very, very close to the lair of the Terrible Dragon, and if *he* gets her we don't need to bother to try to rescue her because there won't be anything left of her to rescue.'

'Oh, no!' Gwydion groaned.

'And if that weren't enough, just around that bush she's hiding behind – not very successfully, either – there is a very large Ravening Wolf. And it looks hungry. Quite honestly, Gwydion, I wonder if it's worth the effort of going to rescue her. By the time we get there she could be just a pile of chewed-up bones. A small pile.'

'But we've got to *try*, Master!' Gwydion pleaded. 'She's my friend! We can't just let her get chomped, can we?'

'*I* certainly could,' Merlin replied, 'since she's caused me a considerable amount of time and trouble by coming here. But I don't expect you could, being a silly, sentimental boy. Oh, very well, we'll give it our best shot.'

Gwydion wasn't very sure what giving it their best shot meant – Merlin was full of sayings that he brought back from other Times, most of which were confusing. But he thought it meant that they were going to try to rescue Betsan.

And then, possibly the most wonderful thing of all happened. Merlin *shapeshifted* first Gwydion, and then himself, into beautiful barn owls. Gwydion took two steps, tripped over his talons and fell on his beak.

'Pay attention, boy,' Merlin squawked. 'Bend your knees like this, and wag your arms. No, not like that, you look like a windmill. Like an owl, you idiot!'

Gwydion thought very hard about owls, then he extended his wonderful, golden brown wings with the white undersides, and gently waved them. To his delight, he *lifted* a few inches into the air! He did it again, and then he was flying round and round the turret, his wings brushing the dark red wall hangings.

'Come on, hurry up, don't waste time messing about,' Merlin ordered, flipping through an arrowslit into the moonlight.

Wheeeee! Gwydion thought, soaring gloriously over the castle battlements.

Yippeeeee! he thought, swooping wondrously over the sleeping fields.

Yum! he thought, hovering hungrily over a fat fieldmouse.

Yuk! he thought. *Boys don't eat mice!*

Then Merlin was dropping down, down, over the darkness of the woods to perch in a tree just outside the Lair of the Terrible Dragon. Below them was a bush. Behind the bush was a girl. Her eyes were tight shut and her hair was tangled and she was wearing strange, blue, shiny boots that came up to her knees. She was hanging on to the bush for dear life.

On the other side of the bush was a very large, very fierce, very hungry, Ravening Wolf. He deserves Capital Letters because he was that sort of Wolf. A medieval sort of wolf, extra-large variety, with slavering jaws and fangs like daggers and lots of stuff like that. He was getting ready to go round the other side of the bush and munch on Betsan. He was quite fond of small humans. They were nice and tender, for a start, and they couldn't run terribly fast so he didn't have to waste too much energy chasing them. And this one looked wonderfully tasty. There wasn't a lot of meat on her, but she'd do for an appetiser.

'Snarl,' said the wolf, getting ready to pounce. 'Snarlsnarlsnarlsnarlgrowwwl!'

'Eek!' said Betsan, opening one eye. 'Help, help, HEEEEEEEELP!' Right at that moment, she'd rather forgotten she was supposed to be Betsan the Brave.

'Come on,' said Merlin, flitting down to the ground between the wolf and Betsan.

Oh, goody! the wolf thought between snarls. *Yummy! Owl for pudding!* Then another owl landed beside the first owl. *Oh,* the wolf thought, *two owls! This is altogether too much! What luck! What an amazingly good meal I'm going to get tonight!*

But then one of the owls shimmered. Its outline went all wavery, and stretched, and grew, and – there was another small human! The wolf decided he'd have the other owl for his appetiser, then the boy as a main course, then the girl for pudding. But then the *other* owl shimmered and shifted, and in its place stood a large person. Normally that wouldn't have bothered the wolf, he'd just have added it to the menu instead of a cheese course, but he recognised *this* person. It wasn't a human, for a start. It was a Magician, and to make matters worse it was Merlin-the-Magician, and one thing that every creature in Ynys Haf knew perfectly well was that you didn't mess with Merlin if you wanted to live a nice, long, comfortable life. Or any sort of a life at all, for that matter.

Speedily the wolf sat back on his haunches, lolloped out his tongue, opened his eyes very wide and wagged his tail. He tried very hard to look like a big old friendly dog. 'Woofywoofwoof?' he said, hopefully, hoping the Master wouldn't realise what he'd been up to.

But the Master did. Merlin bent down until he was nose-to-nose with the Ravening Wolf.

'You know perfectly well, Wolf, that you are not allowed,' he said softly, in Wolfspeak, 'to eat humans. You may eat other creatures, that is the way of wild things. But you may not eat humans, Wolf. Ever.'

'Or Magicians' Apprentices,' Gwydion added quickly.

'Precisely,' Merlin said. 'Now, Ravening Wolf, you have three choices.'

The wolf gulped and nodded. He paid very close attention.

'One, you may turn your tail, make like a tree and leaf . . .' Merlin smiled at his own joke.

The Wolf looked baffled by this.

'Two, you may stay and fight me for this human. If you win, you may eat her.'

Betsan looked appalled – and a shade pale – at this.

'Or, three, I can zap you now and turn you into something very small and furry that every other predator in Ynys Haf might munch on for supper. Now, of the three, I'd personally recomme-'

Too late. The wolf, at approximately the speed of light, decided it was time to go home.

'Gwydion!' Betsan yelled joyfully.

'Shhh!' Gwydion said, grabbing her and slapping his hand over her mouth. 'The lair of the Terrible Dragon is just behind you!'

'I know,' Betsan said airily. 'I just escaped from there. But it's all right. He's already eaten.'

'And the Tylwyth Teg are about. We don't want to run in to *them*, trust me!'

'I did, actually. I got away.'

'You did? Really?'

''Course I did. *Dim problem*. I'm here, aren't I?'

'Perhaps I'd better let the Ravening Wolf come back,' Merlin suggested, 'since you obviously didn't need our help at all.'

'Oh, I did, I did,' Betsan protested. 'I was so scared I couldn't move. That thing was huge, and I just froze. I couldn't move a muscle I was so scared. Thank you for rescuing me! Now, if you'll just be kind enough to show me the way to the Time Door, I've really, really got to get home. My Mam will be worried sick.'

CHAPTER THIRTEEN

'Not so fast, young lady,' Merlin said sternly. 'I think we need to have a talk before you go home. You, Gwydion – and Me. In case you were wondering, I am Great Merlin, Magician to the Dragonking and Protector of Ynys Haf.'

'Thought you might be,' Betsan said, holding out her hand, 'I'm really, really pleased to meet you. I've heard loads about you. Not only from Gwydion, either. There are all sorts of books and stuff about you in my Time.'

'I know,' Merlin said. He bent down to shake Betsan's hand. 'Pleased to meet me, are you? Well, we'll see about that.'

Oh, heck, Gwydion thought glumly. *Now we're for it.*

'But first, we have to get you back to Castell Du.'

And to Betsan's delight, Merlin waved his arms and first Gwydion turned into an owl, then she did, and then Merlin himself. Betsan got the hang of flying rather more quickly than Gwydion had, and as they were soaring into the sky, she thought to herself, *I must remember every second of this to tell Maldwyn. Every single wonderful-amazing-fabulous-unbelievable second.*

The three owls swooped into Merlin's turret and Merlin shifted them back. Betsan stood for a second with her eyes closed and her arms outstretched, remembering the feel of flight. Then she opened them.

'I hope this isn't going to take too long,' she said

firmly. 'My Mam is going to be frantic with worry. She's probably got the police and mountain rescue scouring Blaengwynfi right now.'

'She won't be worried in the slightest,' Merlin said, sitting in his high-backed chair. 'Time is different here. Your mother won't even have noticed you've been missing.'

'Well that's good news, then, isn't it?' Betsan found an empty chair and sat down. 'But I'd still like to go home quickly, please. But before I do I'd probably better tell you that if you think that Great Druid person is still on the beach where you put him, you're wrong.'

Merlin's eyes narrowed and Gwydion winced.

'I'm never wrong,' Merlin said ominously. 'The only way that Druidical menace could have escaped the enchantment I put on him is – oh, you didn't, did you? Tell me you didn't?'

'Sorry, I'm afraid I did,' Betsan said apologetically. 'How was I to know he'd cheat?'

'He always cheats,' Merlin said grimly. 'That's one of the reasons why I keep him safely filed away. Still, it won't take me long to sort him out again.'

Gwydion was amazed. If he'd done something like letting the Great Druid out, Merlin would have been furious, but he was letting Betsan off entirely!

'Anyway,' Betsan went on, 'if you really feel you've got to tell me off, please do it now and get it over with and then I can go home.'

Gwydion shut his eyes and waited for the thunderbolt to strike. When nothing thunderboltish happened, he opened them again. When he looked at Merlin, he was amazed to see that he was *almost* smiling. If *he'd* said something like that, Merlin would have transglommerated him. At least.

'Hmm,' was all Merlin said. He studied Betsan for a few moments over the top of his glasses. 'The problem, Miss Betsan M Price, is that very few humans ever stumble through a Time Door. And when they do, *if* they manage to go back – and most of them don't – we have to make certain that they keep our secrets, otherwise we'd be over-run by the beastly things. Can you even begin to imagine what humans might do to Ynys Haf? Makes a person shudder to think of it.'

'I'll keep it secret, I promise,' Betsan said, but Gwydion noticed that one hand had crept behind her back.

The sneaky little toad thought Gwydion! She was crossing her fingers! That means that every promise she made is backwards! She wasn't promising anything at all! He wondered if he should tell Merlin. Probably not, he decided. If Merlin was so smart, let him work it out for himself.

'I wonder, can I trust you to keep that promise?' Merlin asked sternly.

'Oh, you can,' Betsan said, her eyes gazing at him innocently. 'Really you can!'

'All the same,' Merlin's eyes were definitely twinkling, now. 'All the same, Betsan M Price, I think I should make absolutely sure. Don't you, Gwydion?'

Gwydion didn't say anything.

Before Gwydion escorted Betsan back to the Time Door, Merlin gave Gwydion a tiny bottle. 'Make sure she drinks this before you leave her,' he ordered. 'And

90

bring back the empty bottle so I can use it again! Bottles are expensive.'

'Yessir,' Gwydion said, pocketing the potion.

When they reached the Time Door, Betsan collected the pile of clothes she'd left behind. She didn't put them on, though: the snow on them had melted and they were definitely a bit soggy.

The air shimmered, and there were the two upright stones.

'Well, goodbye, Gwydion,' Betsan said. 'I hope we meet again – only in my Time, if you don't mind! This Time is a bit on the dangerous side.'

'Oh, I'm coming through the Door with you,' Gwydion said. 'Just to see you safe. It's a bit different going back. The important thing to remember is, whatever happens, whatever you do, *don't turn round!* Or you'll be stuck in the Door forever.' He took her hand and they stepped between the stones. They didn't step immediately out into Betsan's Time, as she'd expected. Instead, a long, winding tunnel stretched ahead.

'Come on,' Gwydion said, 'and remember, whatever happens, don't turn round.'

They stepped forward, and instantly they were battered and blasted by a huge wind. It howled and raged around them, and they had to lean forward into it to be able to walk. It was a terrible temptation to turn round, to shield her face from the mighty gusts, but she resisted it. Then, as quickly as it had come, it dropped, and the two of them fell out through the doors – and there they were, on top of the Graig once more.

'Thanks, Gwydion,' Betsan said. She gave him a hug.

Gwydion took the little bottle out of his pocket. 'Merlin says you have to drink this before I leave you,' he said apologetically. 'I think he spotted you had your fingers crossed when you promised.'

'Oh, rats!' She said reluctantly. She took the little bottle and removed the cork and sniffed it. It smelled deliciously of raspberries.

'I'll drink it when you've gone,' she said.

Gwydion shook his head, grinning. 'Can't do that. I've got to take the bottle back. Merlin's into recycling stuff. Waste not, want not, all that, you know.' He knew perfectly well that she wouldn't drink it unless he was standing over her. She was all right, for a girl. She'd been quite brave, really. The stories she'd told about tangling with the giant, the witch, the Tylwyth Teg, the Dragon and the Ravening Wolf – she'd been brave as a hippogriff. Whatever that was.

Betsan the Brave shrugged and raised the bottle to her lips. She emptied the whole lot into her mouth and handed Gwydion the bottle.

'I'll be off then,' Gwydion said. 'See you some Time?'

Betsan nodded, solemnly. She hoped so. Oh, she hoped so.

Gwydion waved once more and stepped back through the Door in Time. The air shimmered, and Gwydion was gone.

And Betsan spat a huge mouthful of raspberry-flavoured Forgetting Spell on the grass on top of the Graig. She spat and spat until only the faintest taste of raspberry lingered in her mouth, and she swallowed not one single drop.

Then she grinned. She couldn't wait to tell Maldwyn!

Betsan the Brave
continues the story that began with
Gwydion and the Flying Wand
and *Magic Maldwyn.*

For even MORE about Gwydion, read:

The Magic Apostrophe
The Island of Summer
Dragonson
Who, me?
Me and My Big Mouth

and coming soon . . .

Decisions – and Dragons

Also by Jenny Sullivan

The Back End of Nowhere
Following Blue Water
Siôn and the Bargain Bee
Two Left Feet